I wasn't brought up like this, thought Dove. I was brought up to be kind and do right. How did Wing turn out bad? She was there with me all along. Why didn't she learn the same things from Mother and Father that I learned?

Or was she there all along? Is she really my vanished twin? Do such things really happen?

Or is she some evil spirit from the ancient past, who came through the skylight, or through the *Venom*, or through whatever terrible powers are out there? Invisible and uncaring?

Or is there no Wing at all? thought Dove Daniel. Just me . . . going insane.

Other Point paperbacks
by CAROLINE B. COONEY

THE PERFUME

Caroline B. Cooney

SCHOLASTIC INC.
New York Toronto London Auckland Sydney

No part of this publication may be reproduced, in whole or in part, or stored in a retrieval system, or transmitted in any form or by any means, electronic, mechanical, photocopying, recording, or otherwise, without written permission of the publisher. For information regarding permission, write to Scholastic Inc., 730 Broadway, New York, NY 10003.

ISBN 0-590-45402-1

12 11 10 9 8 7 6   6 7/9

Printed in the U.S.A.   01

First Scholastic printing, July 1992

Chapter 1

The perfume was advertised once, and only once.

It was enough.

Venom.

The newspaper sprayed outward like a fan, and Dove's hand cramped around it. *Venom* could be read between her fingers like rings.

"Let me see that ad!" cried Connie. She peeled Dove's fingers off as if this were a normal activity: Dove clinging to a newpaper and Connie ripping her hands away.

Dove was a gentle girl, who dressed like her gentle name: soft cottons, soft colors. Folds of pale gray with white lace collars. Her voice was melodious and her friendships were affectionate.

And yet, the word *Venom* attracted Dove like gravity. The newspaper seemed to bite her, like a paper viper.

"Oh, wow!" cried Connie. "It's a new perfume. I love perfumes! What a great name! I have Obsession. I have Poison. I want *Venom*, too." Connie was always full of herself; she would say "I" half a dozen times in every speech. Sometimes Dove was not sure why she and Connie and Luce were such good friends.

"What store is selling it?" asked Luce. She took the newspaper from them both and smoothed it out. "Dry Ice carries it."

"I love Dry Ice," said Connie.

Dry Ice carried the trendiest clothes, the funkiest costume jewelry, the craziest colors, and the sickest T-shirt slogans. Bins of solid carbon dioxide, safely hidden from customers' exploring fingers, wafted clouds of vapor into the air. Through mist, you entered the shop, and once inside you could not see back out. You shopped in fog. When you left, your hair sparkled like morning dew and your skin felt damp and moldy.

Dove never went into Dry Ice without a shiver of fear. The store spoke to her, its voice curling out from under the smoke. *I'm waiting for you, Dove . . . I've always been waiting for you, Dove . . . this store was built for you . . . it's only a matter of time.*

"Let's go to the mall after school," said Connie, "and check out Dry Ice and see what *Venom* looks like."

I cannot be afraid of a store, Dove told herself. I am nearly sixteen.

Of course, being nearly sixteen had not broken Dove's habit of looking under the bed each night to be sure nothing was there. With the hall light on and the bedroom ceiling light on, Dove would crouch in the doorway of her room after brushing her teeth and quickly peer under the bed. No floor-length bed ruffles for Dove. She needed a clear view across the room. It only took a moment, and there never was anything under the bed.

She had not skipped the nightly check in years. You never knew.

"You don't *look* at perfume, silly," said Luce. "You *smell* it." Luce was short for Lucinda, which Luce considered the crummiest name her parents could possibly have selected. ("I might as well be Irmengarde," Luce would say glumly, "or Hulda.")

Luce wore a black knit pullover with a black cotton shirt over it, and black jeans. Luce liked black. Dove owned none. Black was death and night and traps in the dark. Black made Dove's heart shrink, as if her heart were losing weight and would become fragile, and no longer pump blood.

"*Venom*," repeated Connie.

The word clasped Dove like tiny teeth. She almost wanted to scrape it off her mind. Dove shivered, and then shook her head very slightly, freeing it from the word. But instead of leaving her, the word split into two, and bothered her even more, like a cell dividing. *Ven — om.*

"I'll drive, of course," said Luce. Luce had her own car and loved driving. She especially loved driving to the mall, because it involved back roads that twisted and highways with shrieking trucks and tricky left turns across traffic.

Dove was not as fond of the mall as Luce and Connie were, but she enjoyed circling the long halls, taking the sparkly glass escalators up to glittering layers of shops. She would pretend to be rich, going into dress shops to feel the fabrics, and hold the lovely gowns against herself, and stare in the mirrors, with as many dreams as Cinderella.

"I'm not going," said Dove. "Thanks, anyway." She almost thrilled to her own words: how strong she was. What a relief to know she could refuse her best friends. She was no weakling who followed wherever anybody led.

"Because it's Dry Ice?" said Luce, rolling her eyes.

"You're so weird, Dove," said Connie, giggling. "You can't be afraid of a *store*. Come on. I wanna look at *Venom*."

"Smell it," corrected Luce again.

But Connie was right. The perfume would have shape and form and texture. They really would look at it. "I don't think I want to go," said Dove. The creepy tremor came over her again, but on the inside, like something crawling upside down within her skull.

Connie was bored and full of pity, as if spending time on Dove required an effort Connie would shortly stop making. As if Dove were a burden rather than a pleasure. Connie simply propelled Dove ahead of her, toward Luce's car, a prison matron changing cell assignments.

Dove had a weird sense that she did not know Connie: had never known her, in spite of being in class together since nursery school. Connie's long dark hair, neither straight nor curly, but ruffled and tangled, seemed an impenetrable mass of threads, hiding the real Connie. Connie's simple denim shirt, with its gleaming silver buttons, was open at the front to reveal a gaudy T-shirt in hot pink and orange. Connie suddenly seemed very complex to Dove: a girl both tangled and smooth.

A stranger.

"Really," said Dove. "I have a lot of homework. No time to go to the mall." Her hands were cold, her face hot. Her mind felt queerly crowded.

Connie hauled Dove toward Luce's car.

Dove tried to laugh, but the laugh didn't come. "Maybe I'll look in Sears while you're in Dry Ice," said Dove.

"Sears?" repeated Luce. "What — are you insane? Washing machines and lawn mowers? Dove Bar!"

Her nicknames annoyed Dove deeply. "Don't call me Dove Bar," she said.

"Then don't be an idiot," said Connie, who had never received a nickname and was jealous of a friend who had so many. "Just come with us."

Luce's car was a tiny little thing: as flimsy as a can of peas and about the same color. The seats were extremely hard, as if the assembly line had forgotten to pad the metal — just glued vinyl straight to the steel. Luce drove fiercely, shifting gears like throwing sticks of dynamite. Connie fidgeted with the radio. She was a radio freak who was never satisfied and punched her way through stations.

Dove sat in the back, tossed up and down on the unyielding seat no matter how tightly she yanked the safety belt.

The parking lot of the mall was jammed.

To Dove, parking lots were like cemeteries.

Empty spaces were white rectangles waiting for metal coffins.

Once she had gone to day camp. Every morning the bus took the children from the pickup on South Main six miles to the camp at Slick Lake. Its route passed a cemetery. "Don't breathe!" somebody would shout. "It's bad luck to breathe when you're going past dead people."

Dove had never been able to hold her breath long enough. She would always have to breathe before they were past the tombstones.

"What will happen to me?" she had said anxiously to her mother one day.

"Oh, Dovey, don't be such a dumbo," her mother said crossly. "That's the oldest nonsense in the book. That's like being afraid there's something under the bed."

This did not comfort the child who knew — had always known — that someday there would indeed be something under the bed.

Full parking lots, on the other hand, were doom: the end of the world.

Metal boxes, which only a moment ago had been full of people and chatter and beating hearts, were now locked, hard and identical.

Dove could not bear things that matched. Identical objects seemed to accuse her of some crime, because she could not distinguish between them. She could not look at them. She knew she would spend a portion of her adult life wandering through huge parking lots, trying to remember where she had left her car, what her car looked like, why she had ever come to the mall, what the purpose of her life was.

I am Dove Daniel, she said to herself. I am a nice person. I have brown hair and brown eyes and Timmy O'Hay thinks I'm cute. Of course he hasn't done anything about it, but that's a boy for you. I don't have to worry about the purpose of my life and I don't have to worry about how to find the car afterward, because Luce always remembers where she left the car.

In the front seat, Connie fluffed her tangled hair off her neck, and Luce tipped the visor to study herself in the mirror on the back of it.

For a moment Dove did not know who they were. She seemed to be looking at photographs in somebody else's yearbook: the backs of anonymous teenagers.

They parked. Luce tilted back the passenger seat to let Dove crawl out.

"Let's look in the pet shop," Dove offered. She wanted to touch long-haired dogs, listen to screeching parrots, watch shimmering fish.

"No, dummy, listen up," said Connie. "We're going into Dry Ice. *Venom.* Isn't that perfect? Don't you love it? *Venom.*" She said the *V* long and hard. A wasp stinging. Dove was stung by fear.

"Is there an antidote?" asked Luce.

Luce and Connie giggled.

"Serum to save yourself from your own perfume," agreed Connie. "We should write the manufacturer."

They were in the mall, passing the neon-bright store guide, passing the smells of pizza and cinnamon and grease from the Food Court, gliding up the escalator whose glass walls were caught with diamond sparkles.

Toward the third level, the vapor from Dry Ice oozed out into the mall.

A cologne of terror invaded Dove's mouth. "If I go in there, I won't dare breathe," she said to her friends. "If that perfume goes into my lungs, it'll get into my bloodstream."

The vapor worked its way toward Dove. It wrapped itself around Dove's ankles and she kicked at it, trying to free herself.

Luce howled with laughter. "You are so *weird*, Dove Bar!"

They pushed her into the shop first. The queer thick damp of the carbon dioxide vapor steamed her hair.

Dove could hardly see the display cases. If there were salespeople, they were invisible in the thick fog of their own making.

Her lungs screamed for air. Her heart hurt and her head ached, demanding oxygen. Good old breathing material.

Connie was trying on the new perfume.

Dove could actually see the fragrance coming,

borne on the sick white vapor from the dry ice. She could taste it. It went right to her chest, leaping across the barriers of cell and membrane, and entering her blood.

It wrapped itself around her heart.

Venom.

It was primitive and dark.

It went back before history. Before civilization or time. Before sanity.

Let go my heart, thought Dove. Please! Let go my heart.

"What a great container!" exclaimed Connie, holding up the bottle.

The glass was translucent, like an unpolished diamond, hiding its contents. It was shaped like a snake. Connie held it to her chest, and Dove thought of Egypt, and pyramids, and Cleopatra holding an asp to her bosom, standing still and elegant while it bit her. Dying of the venom.

"I don't really like the smell, though, do you?" asked Connie.

"It's interesting," said Luce, frowning, "but not . . . " Luce had no words for this scent. She said, "*You* know . . . " which is what people say when they don't, and neither do you. "It's not very attractive, is it?" she said finally.

Dove reached for the open snake. She told her hand not to, but it went forward anyway, clasped the glass, and lifted it to her face.

Two vapors entered her body: the dry ice and the perfume.

"Are you going to get it, Dove Bar?" asked one of her friends.

She could not tell them apart anymore. Nor remember their names.

The store gloated. *We knew we would get you*, said the store. *Didn't we tell you it was only a matter of time?*

Dove felt that her life had been a prelude to this moment.

Had never counted until this breath of perfume. *Venom.*

Whooo venom? thought Dove. What bit me?

And she knew that tonight, at last, there would be something under the bed.

Chapter 2

Two hundred sharp-edged, identical condominiums.

Tailored gray and white, the condominiums marched up and over a steep jut of land, from which both sunrise and sunset could be admired.

Sky Change Hills.

It was one of those foolish development names, like Rockrimmon Valley, when there were no rocks, no rims, and no valley. Or Fox Hollow, when there had been neither foxes nor hollows in two generations.

And yet the sky did change, and it seemed to Dove that it changed more often and more vividly than anywhere else, the way autumn leaves in New England are more scarlet, or more orange, than anywhere else.

Today the sky was also gray, with rims of pale clouds, like swathes of uncut satin, softly folding to the horizon. The color match between the condominium units and the sky was so exact that one filtered into the other with only a change in texture: hard building, soft sky.

The sun must still exist in the universe, but there was no sign of it: No piece of sky was bright; nothing glowed; nothing struggled to pierce the gray.

Luce, as always, let Dove out at the narrow guard box. Her car was so low-slung, she couldn't drive over the speed bumps. Nobody ever manned the guard box. It was just there to hold flowerpots. It was early in the spring, and the flowerpots had been planted but had not bloomed; but at least the pots were terra-cotta, a warm dark Mediterranean brown.

Connie got out to let Dove out. Dove emerged with her heavy navy-blue book bag in one hand, and a tiny shopping bag in the other. It was made of heavy slick paper with the Dry Ice emblem on it, and the handles were silky cords with tassels. White tissue paper peeked out the top, brushing against Dove's wrist. The perfume bottle hardly weighed a thing.

"I can't believe you actually bought the *Venom*," said Connie. "I mean, I love the name of it, too, but a person wouldn't actually wear that stuff."

"Subtle, Connie," said Luce, giggling. "She's not going to wear it, are you, Dove Bar? If she did, she'd have to change her whole wardrobe and her whole personality. That is not the perfume for a cooing dove."

I'm the same color as the sky and the buildings, thought Dove. I might vaporize even as we stand here, diffuse like the perfume into all that gray.

" 'Bye!" called Luce, revving the engine.

"See ya!" shouted Connie, rolling down the window and waving.

Dove seemed unable to think of anything to say, as if Dry Ice had drained away her vocabulary. She smiled at them vaguely, but they didn't see, didn't care, were already driving off, consumed with whatever new topic they had launched.

I'm all alone, thought Dove.

And yet she felt strangely occupied, like a couch with a person sitting there.

The condominiums seemed to look at each other and shrug knowingly, exchanging glances above Dove's head.

But they were new, these buildings. They had no history, no past. How could they know anything at all? They had lived through only one winter.

Like row upon row of identical twins, every Levolor blind lying evenly inside every neat window, the units were bland as pieces of paper.

Not one of them was a home. They were a huge indistinguishable litter of front doors.

Dove walked among them like a stranger selling cosmetics.

Where do I live? thought Dove, trembling.

Dark doors looked at her, no expressions on them, no interest; slabs of wood painted slate gray.

The air was raw and mean. Spring had collapsed; had let winter pierce it like a pin in a balloon. There was no safety in spring. Spring could double back and vanish into winter without giving notice. I hate seasons, thought Dove. You cannot trust a season.

She swallowed.

What number is our unit? she thought, lost in her own home territory.

Even the numbers seemed identical. Too high. Too many digits. Was it 11881? Was it 11331? Was it 88118?

She walked for some time. She could not tell if she had circled the entire complex once, or twice, or if she were only halfway around. She could not even tell if she had been anywhere at all.

Suddenly, her heart did something anatomically impossible. It made a double beat. She looked down at her chest.

The heart did it again.

It was not that her pulse was going faster.

Her heart had doubled.

Dove set down her book bag and extracted her purse.

Seventh grade — the first year Dove carried a purse — she had been so thrilled with the opportunity to bring necessities with her that she had used a purse large enough for her entire life: an overnight bag of a purse. The joy of lugging this around palled and now, each season, her purse grew smaller. As she drew closer to sixteen — magical number; infinitely older than callow fifteen — she was down to a slim rectangle on a thin leather rope: a bright tapestry of colors, like a pile of autumn leaves. These were not her usual bland colors, and they gave her hope that the real Dove, the bright and shimmering Dove, might emerge on that magic birthday and stun the world.

I don't want to be a gray old Dove Bar and blend in with the sky and the soap, she thought. I don't want to be the kind of girl who can't even find her own front door. I don't want to be pathetic.

Inside the little handbag was her emergency notification card, with her address neatly printed. She was 11844. How could she have forgotten such a crucial thing?

Her heart double-timed again, and Dove said, "Stop that."

A woman Dove had not noticed, stooping over her one blossoming shrub to pluck its one remaining blossom, stared at Dove. "It's my bush," the woman said defensively. "I can pick the flower if I want."

"I meant my heart," explained Dove. "It's gotten away from me."

"Hearts do that," said the woman. She smiled gently, remembering a love of her own.

But there was no love involved in Dove's double beat.

Dove backed up until she found 11844.

Her key fit.

She went in.

Like every other unit at Sky Change Hills, it featured white walls, soaring ceilings, long-chained chandeliers, and layers of narrow balconies.

The nubbly carpet that covered the five staggered levels of floor and stair was also gray, with black and white speckles. It reminded Dove of parking lots.

Identical twin couches were covered with white leather. A large low coffee table, like a slab of smooth fake granite, hunched between them. Two long swings of black metal arced over the couches to provide reading lights.

How neat, how sparse, how *anybody* this living room was.

If her family were to move away, nobody would know the difference. They had left no mark. The condo was more like a tin can than a house; any old vegetable or soup could be packaged in it. It could always be recycled.

She walked as slowly as a burglar wondering what to steal.

The stairs were a bright, space-taking well of carpeted steps. They led down to the playroom in which nobody played, and down below that, to the garage in which two cars would be parked when her parents got home from work. Up the steps was balcony one, and up more steps was her parents' suite, then balcony two, and finally her own bedroom.

She tilted her head to stare up the shaft that was the stairwell and skylight.

The sky showing in the skylight was blue.

But —

Dove turned, frowning, to look back outside.

Through the narrow, half-tilted window blinds, she could see the opposite matching condos and a long slice of sky.

Gray, like a flock of lost doves.

Sky Change Hills.

It must have meant today. For indigo blue, thick

as pudding, filled the sky in the skylight.

Eyes locked on the blue square, Dove began climbing the stairs to the top. To balcony three, where she almost never went.

It was supposed to be an "eyrie," an eagles' nest.

She was a Dove. She nested in her own room.

Her room was pastel: pale chalky hues like lemon and dusty rose. She yearned for as much color as a Hawaiian beach: for gaudy posters, bright scarves, slaps of primary color paint, richly hued sheets, and rows of shoes in purple, yellow, green, blue, scarlet, hot pink, chartreuse. . . . But she never bought those. They frightened her, as if she would not be Dove any longer were she to break forth in brightness.

Nothing in Dove's room matched. Nothing was even. Nothing came in pairs. Nothing was folded with square corners. Identical things were impossible to endure.

But she did not enter the safety of her own room.

She went up toward the sky, like a bird about to fly.

Her heart was going crazy, beating double, supplying so much blood to her system that it was enough for two.

Balcony three was carpeted in the nubbly gray that waffled up the stairs and balconies, and here at the top, it could not stop itself, but even covered the walls, forming little steplike seats.

This was a "retreat."

Not that anybody had ever retreated there. It

was too open. When they retreated — which in her family was always — they went to their own rooms and shut their doors.

Dove set her book bag on one of the step seats.

Next to it, she set her package from Dry Ice.

There was a handle on the skylight. It was a working window. Carefully, Dove released the lock. She put one hand on the handle and turned it easily. One full turn did not move the skylight. A second full turn and the skylight lifted perceptibly. On the third full turn, the glass began to straighten itself and tilt upright, and then Dove could stand and touch the sky.

The sky that was blue . . . the sun that was yellow . . . the air that was warm with spring . . . on a day that was gray and chilly.

Her head stuck out of the top of the condo.

There was nothing in sight.

Not a rooftop.

Not a treetop.

Not a plane or a bird.

Not a horizon or a view.

Just blue, blue sky.

Some other world entirely; some other time and space.

The bottle of perfume had tumbled out. It lay like a crystal snake on the soft rug.

Venom.

Dove lifted the perfume.

The stopper was crystal.

A simple cylinder, glittering.

She rested the bottle against her cheek, and it *was* dry ice, burning her with its terrible temperature. It branded her face. She yanked it from her skin and held it away from herself, toward the blue, blue sky.

A warm shaft of wind curled down the skylight. She could almost see the wind: a blue flag wrapping around her wrist. She shook the wind off her arm. But since she was still holding the perfume bottle by the stopper, the bottle dropped, while the stopper remained in her hand.

The perfume fell gently to the cushion of the carpet, its snake neck curled so that not a drop spilled.

But its scent . . . oh, its scent . . . like the wind, *Venom* slipped out of the bottle diffused through the air, settled on Dove's hair, rested on Dove's hand, filled her body.

Her lungs and heart and brain breathed *Venom*.

As she had almost seen the wind, she almost saw something else, too: almost saw another person, almost felt another life.

No body. No flesh. No form.

Invisible as fragrance.

But nevertheless, it was there.

And full of . . .

. . . *venom*.

Chapter 3

In the morning, Dove felt a flutter inside her head.

It was a gentle movement, a bird shifting position in the nest at night. She shuddered slightly when the feeling stopped. Stood quite still, not wanting to feel that again.

She felt it again.

Something was brushing up against the inside of her skull.

Dove brushed her hair very hard, to push the feeling away.

The feeling increased.

Dove rushed downstairs, hoping to find a parent, but they had left, of course; each had a long commute, in different directions, and they began their days early.

Dove's mother, whose car had a telephone and a fax machine, would be putting her lipstick on at the red light and making her first business call of the day at a comfortable sixty miles an hour on the turnpike heading north.

Dove's father would be using his time well: This

was very important to Dove's father. He was learning another language from a set of expensive cassette tapes. Dove thought it was Japanese; last year he had learned German. He looked most odd when driving, his mouth curling around foreign syllables, with nobody in the passenger seat to be talking to.

In the empty kitchen, Dove's head was full.

Like a full stomach — as if she had eaten too much.

But in her head?

Had she thought too much?

Studied too much?

Daydreamed too much?

Her head was stuffed and cramped.

Dove suddenly hit the side of her head with the bottom of her palm. It seemed to work. Her mind settled down, like a bed being made: sheets momentarily fluffed and then resting.

"Oooh, boy, do I need breakfast," muttered Dove to herself. She fixed something very sturdy: instant oatmeal black with raisins.

The raisins stared at her like eyes.

She put a spoonful to her mouth and thought, If I eat this, my stomach will be full of eyes.

She went to school hungry.

In school, Dove could see and recognize all her friends. She was able to say hello and respond normally when they said, "Hey, how are you?" But in the thickness of her head she felt cramped and distant, as though she actually occupied some other place, and had to communicate with her friends long distance.

The flutter in her head got up and looked around.

Dove wanted to scratch the inside of her brain. She knotted her fingers to keep from ripping out her hair.

This is how stags feel, thought Dove, when they first get antlers, and have to rub themselves against the trees to get the velvet off.

What would they do if she rubbed her head against the classroom walls?

"The brain, you see," said the biology teacher, "is similar to an onion."

Dove detested onions. If you chopped them, your hands smelled. If you cooked them — and the Daniels often did; her father was fond of small white onions in thick white sauce — they were like baby golf balls soaked in glue.

"There are also many layers to the brain," said the biology teacher.

Dove connected with that. Her brain *did* have many layers. She could feel the flutter inside her head lifting each brain layer, like blankets on a bed, deciding where to rest for the night.

At the table they shared, Laurence moaned slightly. Laurence was adorable to look at, but tiresome to be around. He had been that way since they were little kids, and was unlikely to change. Girls were always getting crushes on Laurence and then changing their minds. Laurence was proof that looks were not everything. "Wrong," murmured Laurence. "There is nothing layered about the brain. Convoluted, yes. Layered, no."

Dove raised her hand.

The teacher, always eager to coach an inquiring mind, recognized her. "Yes, Dove?" he said happily.

"You know how sometimes babies are born with two of something?" said Dove. "An extra heart or an extra kidney?"

"An extra eyeball," agreed Timmy O'Hay, pretending to have one. Timmy was the opposite of Laurence: tiresome to look at but terrific to be around. After a while you forgot that Timmy was rumpled and wrinkled and just enjoyed him.

The teacher sighed. "I have never actually heard of extra hearts, Dove, but yes, sometimes there are major deformities at birth."

"Have you ever heard of an extra brain?" she said.

"Dove, please. Let's be logical here. There isn't room in a skull for an extra brain."

"Sure there is," asserted Timmy. "Take Laurence here. The trick is that both brains are very small, see. They don't take you very far. Won't be long, Laurence's brains will fold up shop. It'll be an institution for Laurence, a bed with rails and a nurse with injections to keep him calm."

"Timmy," said the teacher tiredly.

The fluttering had been replaced by footsteps. A second person was walking around inside her head. Insectlike. As if her second person had more than two legs; had eight, perhaps.

"What if you really did have a second person inside you?" said Dove.

"If you really did have a second person inside of you," said the teacher, "you would receive a mental diagnosis. Schizophrenia, perhaps. You would be on heavy-duty, industrial-strength medication, and very probably live out your unfortunate years in the state institution to which Timmy hopes to send Laurence."

The class laughed.

"Oh," said Dove. She decided against describing what was going on inside her skull. The world did not sound sympathetic.

Her next class was ancient history.

It was an elective, for people who had done especially well in American history the year before. She could have taken current world, but since Dove's family watched the news every night during supper — they never talked; the only talking done in her house was by television commentators — Dove felt too acquainted with the current world already. She opted for the ancient world, and now they were doing Egypt.

A sharp hard pain began in the exact center of Dove's skull.

The second person had taken up residence. The person was hard, like a piece of gravel in a shoe. Just as the biology teacher had said, there was not enough room up there. Dove's mind was shoved against the wall of her skull, her thoughts pressed closer together, like recycled newspapers jammed into a container on the sidewalk.

"There is evidence," said the teacher, "that the ancient Egyptians did brain surgery. Skulls in tombs have been found in which holes were drilled, probably to relieve pressure from brain tumors. Or possibly it was thought that during a psychotic episode, the evil influence could be given an escape hatch. The technique is called *trepanning*."

Dove could visualize this perfectly.

There would be a surgeon in a white linen skirt and a golden necklace shaped like a scarab. He would have a long drill, which he would hand-turn, and the patient would be fastened down on a board, head resting on a stone pillow, and the Egyptian surgeon would drill a hole into the skull.

What a relief it must have been to the patient.

Dove wanted to lie on one of those Egyptian couches and have her head drilled. Get this second person out of her head.

It would probably be a relief to the second person as well. An escape hatch.

Perhaps a lid could be put on: a scalp flap.

No, because then the second person could come back in. The second person would treat the skull like a hotel. Come back when he felt like it and tuck himself in.

Dove touched her hair, feeling for the soft spot where the hole could be drilled.

Through the silk of her hair, the rubberiness of her scalp, and the hard bone of her head, Dove felt an answer.

Dove did not need to drill holes.

The person inside was going to come out by itself.

Chapter 4

Night fell.

Where there had been gray, there was black. Where there had been soft edges, there were no edges at all.

Only darkness.

Dove was aware of her parents as she had never been before.

First, there was her mother. Not very old. Thirty-six. As slim and fit as she'd been in high school, Dove's mother still looked like a teenager. Brilliant in math, she was a busy accountant for a tax firm. How boring and strict the numbers seemed to Dove; how demanding and how dull taxes must be. But Dove's mother loved her clients, sorting out their business expense problems and giving them better ideas.

Dove thought that her mother's brain was filled with numbers instead of words, and that it clicked like an adding machine.

Dove's mother detested cooking and rarely did any.

Her great pleasure was clothing. She had taken a job in a large, polished firm because it was a great excuse to dress beautifully and differently and expensively every day.

Dove loved her mother.

Then there was her father. His body had thickened over the years, and he was constantly on a diet. He stuck to each diet by day and caved in by night, when it was nothing for him to consume four or five desserts. He was always joining a health club or starting up a swimming membership, or taking up running, but he would lose interest within a month. He worked for the phone company, and unlike Mother, Father did not like his job. He had never liked his job, and it was a mystery to Dove why he stayed with it. It was a mystery to Father, too, and reaching for that line of desserts seemed to be linked with the eight grim hours of a job he loathed. Dove could not understand why he did not quit and find something better.

Dove loved her father deeply.

And yet she was not close to her parents.

They rarely chatted, or talked of intimate things, or shared stories of what happened that day. It seemed to Dove that her family lay on the surface of family life; they shared a house, a dinner table, and a television screen.

She did not know who her mother's best friend was, or what her father did on those days he came home late, or what made them love each other.

More and more, as Dove grew up, she saw that

these parents of hers were not only total strangers to her, they were total strangers to each other.

That night, she asked for a story.

Her mother's elegant eyebrows lifted. "A story?" repeated her mother, amused.

"About when I was little," said Dove eagerly. She loved stories about herself. There weren't many. She had not been an exciting child. "Or when you and Father were in college," she added, giving them an out. Their own lives would be an easier story for them.

Her parents sighed slightly, privately. Separately they seemed to remind themselves that every parent must expect to exert him- or herself occasionally. Dove's mother glanced at her watch. Dove's father rested his magazine at an angle from which he could still read the large print of the captions, if not actually the articles.

She knew that they did not think of themselves as Dove's Mother and Dove's Father. They thought of themselves as Jan and Rob. Sometimes she thought of them that way, too.

"Well, of course," her father began, "we had expected two. They said your mother was going to have twins."

The familiar sadness of having disappointed her parents even before birth filtered through Dove. The sadness felt as visible as the vapor from Dry Ice, damp and infinite.

"Ultrasound showed two," said her father, smiling at the memory, "and we bought two of everything: two bassinets and a double carriage. It seemed very efficient to have two at a time." Her father approved of efficiency.

What had happened to the extra carriage and bassinet? For that matter, what had happened to hers? Her parents kept nothing. There were no keepsakes in this immaculate condominium, no attic, no cardboard boxes of the past, no trunks or forgotten drawers full of interesting memorabilia.

"One daughter would be Dove," said her father. "Soft and gentle and cooing with affection." He surprised Dove by resting his hand on hers, and for a moment the vapors lifted and she was safe and dry.

"The other would have been Wing," added her mother. "Beating free and flying strong."

Hard to imagine such methodical people thinking of romantic unusual names. You would have expected them to utilize names like Emily and Mary, which parents had leaned on and been sure of over centuries.

Wing and Dove.

Suddenly the two names were horrid. Almost evil.

A Dove was whole. A complete bird, a complete child. Whereas a Wing — that was just a portion. A limb, so to speak, wrenched off, and lost forever.

How could they have done that? thought Dove. How could they have chosen such a set of names?

For how could a Wing be born alone? Fly free and be strong! Quite the opposite. Without its identical match, a Wing was nothing.

No wonder it wasn't born, thought Dove, how could it be?

"I still think about Wing sometimes," offered her mother.

This was not part of the story. Because Dove never knew what her mother was thinking, she leaned forward, hoping to catch another molecule of understanding about this unknown woman who had given birth to her.

"We used to sing to Wing and Dove," said her mother, smiling now, "your father and I." She did not look at Dove, but into the past, fifteen years ago. She seemed more interested in Wing, who did not exist, than in Dove, who did. "We were sure Wing and Dove could hear, *in utero*, so we'd read aloud from important books. We'd play great music on the stereo, and oh! how carefully I would eat! We wanted Wing and Dove to emerge from the womb sophisticated and intellectual and perfect."

The order of the names, too . . . Wing first. Dove second.

I'm a second, thought Dove. A factory second. Irregular.

"However," said Father, shrugging, "Wing split."

"Split?" repeated Dove, and suddenly, the familiar story became unutterably horrible.

She thought of Wing, safe in the tiny sea of their mother's body, listening to her strange name being called from the other side of the flesh. She heard Wing whisper to herself — No, I don't think so. I'm not going to be born.

Splitting. The word was evil.

"How did you know it was Dove who was still

around," asked Dove, "and not Wing?"

"Well, it was very strange," said her mother, "but we never had a question about that. Dove was born and Wing vanished."

The phenomenon was actually called that: vanishing twin syndrome.

If they did not lose interest in the conversation, her parents would move into the biology lecture portion of the story. Twins were often predicted in the first weeks of pregnancy but failed to grow after all.

Her parents lost interest, as they always did, and sat silently engaged in their own thoughts and television shows.

The moment of closeness had vanished like the other twin.

Dove trembled with the heaviness of being alone.

Do other people feel this alone, even with their families in the room? she thought. Or do I know in my bones that I am missing a sister, and therefore I am more alone than most girls? What would I have done with her if I had had her? What would she have done with me?

If she never lived, how could she have split?

Where did she vanish *to*?

That night, Dove did not look under her bed.

All her life, she had looked because the truth of the event was that she knew it was safe to look. There could not really be anything bad under there. Nothing was under any bed except carpet and lost socks.

But it was no longer safe to look.

There *was* something bad under there.

There was something bad under her entire fifteen years.

Wing.

By the next ancient history class, Dove no longer believed that Wing had vanished.

Wing had been there all along, waiting. Incubating like a disease.

Wing was ready to come out.

Would she drill her own hole, this twin her mother still thought about?

Would she slide out of Dove's head like a breath of air through her nostrils?

Would she be vapor or would she have a body of flesh?

Whose body would Wing use?

Or did she have one of her own stored up?

Dove saw an unused body under the bed, waiting to be dressed and taken out for a walk.

"Pyramids, Dove?" said the teacher.

The unused body seemed to be Dove herself, and she felt herself walking away from herself, like a ghost leaving town.

Dove wet her lips.

"For your next presentation, Dove," said the teacher, with infinite patience. "Do you want to be on the pyramids committee or the Nile committee?"

"Oh, pyramids," said Dove.

Chapter 5

Pyramids, indeed, were quite interesting.

Dove had known that they were more than tombs — they were houses for the afterlife of kings — but she had not pictured such large interior rooms. Nor had she realized that each cavern full of treasure and furnishing was decorated: zigzag painted ceilings and grape-leaf 'wallpaper.'

All the books on pyramids were wonderfully illustrated: amazing color photographs gleaming in gold and hot with turquoise. She turned page after page, staring at the 'house' in which a dead king had lived for five thousand years.

The person in her head shifted position; it was like gravel spurting out from under car tires. Pebbles shot against Dove's mind.

She knocked on her skull as if on a door, as if she could tap out the code for open sesame.

Was the inside of her own head a sort of round pyramid? The tomb in which this other creature had been kept for fifteen years?

And what was it like inside, where that second person lived?

Were the walls painted?

Were the ceilings interesting?

Dove clung to her head, pressing down with all ten fingers. Am I trying to extract the second person, she thought, or suffocate it?

In one of the deepest onion layers of her thinking, she knew that it was Wing in there: She knew she could not bear to acknowledge this, that her own sister had been "camping out" in her brain, a parasite of her head. She could not use the name.

If I were her, thought Dove, would that make me mad? What can she be like after all this time? Do I want to know? Do I want her out?

Would I be better off with her living inside me, rattling around like a marble in a wooden box?

Dove sat on the carpeted stairs outside her bedroom. She liked the open feeling of the condo when she sat there: steps stretching up and down, airy spaces all around. From this perch she could see no floors and no furniture, only white walls and wide windows.

The sky was gray again.

Heavy chilled angry gray.

Solid gray.

A sky without laughter or relief or softness.

A sky full of rage.

And a balcony full of sound.

Sound rushed through Dove's head as if she were wearing earphones with the volume up. She could not name the sound. It was not music nor footsteps, not gale winds nor rising tides.

It's the sounds of the insides of pyramids, thought Dove, when the priests closed the entrances and the tunnels forever, when the last fresh air went stale and the last fraction of light went dark.

She stood up.

The person inside her needed more space, was going to stretch down from her skull into her spine. Into her shoulders and down her arms. Perhaps envelop her heart.

Now she looked below into the living room, with its pristine tailored gray and white identical twin couches. Did her mother miss Wing right down to the furniture?

Dove's heart was not merely doubling now. Not merely having twins. Her heartbeat was tripling. Quadrupling. Giving birth. *To what?*

Soundless on the thick carpet, Dove twisted and turned and stumbled, trying to get free of the sound and the space the person in her head was taking up.

The person in her head was screaming now.

Dove could not make out the words, but she could feel the frenzy: Her brain was being kicked, beaten, bitten.

"Stop it!" screamed Dove.

The person in her head hurled itself against the prison of Dove's skull.

"Stop it!" screamed Dove. She backed into her

room, into the soft colors and soothing lights. At the makeup table, she sat panting, staring at herself in the mirror, trying to see if it showed. If there were two people reflected there.

Not two, but three of her looked back.

Dove screamed and quite clearly she heard the person inside laughing.

Dove hung onto the edges of the makeup table, where the ruffled skirt was tacked to the rim. She felt the cotton against her sweaty palms.

It's all right, Dove said to herself. This is a makeup mirror. It's always reflected three of me. I like it that way. Easier to see how I look from the side.

She brushed her hair to calm herself.

She brushed on a little more rose blush to calm herself.

A bit of lip gloss.

And then her hand lingered over the perfume bottle that lay like a coiled snake between her mascara wand and her crystal earrings.

The voice of Dry Ice spoke to her, its voice curling out from under the smoke of her thoughts. *I'm waiting for you . . . I've always been waiting for you . . . it's only a matter of time.*

Time sifted through her fingers like fog.

Slowly, gracefully, like a ballerina before a vast audience, Dove's hand drew a path over the bottle of *Venom.* Her fingers closed on the stopper. Slowly, gently, carefully, she slid it up. It ceased to be a stopper. It was an opener.

The scent rose in the condominium, a scent as

old as the insides of pyramids. A scent as dark and unforgiving as the death of kings.

Dove breathed it in, and it circled inside her; circled where air could not go; circled through her mind and thoughts as well as her blood and bone.

Venom.

The sick tug of gravity, stretching back into prehistory. Ancestors, genes — the hidden evil warped history of herself.

No! thought Dove, I am a nice person! There is nothing in me that is evil or warped! I am good, I am —

Dove breathed out.

A terrible thickness came from her lungs, as if she were exhaling life.

She tried to cry out, but her lungs were full of something.

She tried to steady herself, but her hands were fighting off something. The flapping and the fluttering beat against her hearing and her thinking and her breathing.

She felt as if moths were clustering behind her skin, battering themselves against her brain.

And then it was over.

The inside of her head was quiet.

Spacious.

Roomy.

There was nobody in there except Dove herself.

Wing had emerged.

Chapter 6

At first, Wing was invisible. Dove kept looking for her, knowing that she was there somewhere. But she could not seem to see her.

Then Dove realized that Wing was there all right: The problem was that Wing was occupying the only body available. Dove's.

Dove was the invisible one.

It was Wing who dashed down the stairs, leaped from one level to another, bounced on the bed, hurdled banisters like a gymnast, slammed a heavy door, and ran her hands under cold water, flicking the droplets on her face.

Dove did not feel it. It was her face, her skin, her hands — and she did not feel it.

"I always wondered how this felt," said another person's voice, higher pitched, more fluty than Dove's. Wing. Wing who now possessed the body while Dove bounced around in the back of the skull.

Dove had not actually dissolved.

It was more that she was taking up a different

kind of residence. Dove would have to accompany Wing, just as Wing, for fifteen years, had had to go with Dove.

She could still look out of her own eyes, though; she still seemed to have use of parts of the body. Everything was inside out. As if she was using binoculars backwards, Dove could see a tiny little bed, a miniature desk, and an infinitely small perfume bottle. It was her bed, and her desk, and her perfume, but far far away. Diminished. Unreachable.

Wing reached out and retrieved the perfume instead of Dove. Dove no longer had hands to do anything with. No, thought Dove, seized with dread. This cannot be happening to me. You can't go through life without hands. Without a body. Without —

"I thought you were never coming," Wing said to the bottle, as if she and the bottle were old friends, had known each other for years.

Inside the head, Dove whimpered.

Wing unstoppered the *Venom* again, waving it gently beneath her nose. Dove drowned in the scent, sloshed in it; it was like a lake and Dove a mere feather upon it.

Stop! thought Dove desperately. Please stop! I don't want this. I'm a nice person. Please . . . stop . . . p . l . e . a . s . e . . . .

At last Wing closed the perfume bottle. *"Venom! I am Venom."* Her whisper dissolved in the air as the fragrance had, and diffused throughout the condominium.

Wing smiled, and through Wing's eyes Dove saw the smile reflected three times in the makeup mirror, an evil smile.

Dove shivered.

"Stop that," said Wing irritably, hitting her head.

They had reversed themselves. If she fluttered enough, she could bother Wing. I am the whole dove, she thought, complete, whereas she was only a part. I can bother her much much more than she was able to bother me.

But Dove was not ready to bother Wing.

She wanted to know Wing.

This was, after all, her sister. Blood of her blood.

I could watch her, thought Dove. I'm safe inside here; I'm a passenger, like a wallet in a purse. But I want to talk to her.

"We're both in your mouth," said Wing. "Although I have no interest in hearing you speak. I've gotten headaches from you for so long now. Furthermore you have nothing interesting to say, Dove."

So Wing knew Dove's thoughts. Or heard them. Or perhaps had them herself, because perhaps Wing was Dove, and Dove was Wing. Was I always two people? thought Dove. Am I still two? Is there just one of us?

What is happening?

Who am I?

Am I anything at all? I'm not here.

Dove, looking out through the eyes, tried speaking through the mouth. It worked. "Why are you here?" said Dove. It was her own voice, an alto voice, fuller and friendlier than the sharp soprano Wing used.

"I am *Venom*," said Wing, "I am poison."

Dove glanced toward the perfume bottle, but it was not in her range of vision. She could not make the head turn where she wanted: Wing was using the head.

I don't have a head, thought Dove.

She found herself wondering if Timmy O'Hay could still like a girl who did not have a head.

"You don't know how I have longed for freedom," said Wing. "I loathe you, you know. If we had both been born, I would have done away with you." Wing frowned momentarily. "Of course, I can't do that now, since we occupy the same body."

"You loathe me?" whispered Dove. "But — I'm — I guess I'm — your sister. What's wrong with me?"

Wing flung herself backward onto Dove's bed. Dove felt as if she were in an elevator falling twenty stories. "All those virtues," said Wing. "You're so boring. You're always running around being kind and generous and thoughtful and careful."

"I think I'm rather nice," said Dove timidly.

Wing laughed, and her laugh was broken cubes, clinking from a tipped glass, spilling on a hard floor. "*I'm* not. Take away the *n* of nice. Then you have me. I am ice."

Dove shivered again, which made Wing hit her head to stop the fluttering. But the skull was thick, and the smack simply gave Dove another shiver from the outside in.

"I was unfit, you know," said Wing. "The maternal body often discards an unborn that is unfit. The maternal body does not like to spend nine months on a creature whose chromosomes add up incorrectly."

The maternal body.

She means Mother, thought Dove. She tried to keep her thoughts down in the onion layer where Wing would not share them. She had not realized how precious the privacy of the mind is. I've lost my mind, she thought. Literally. Somebody else has my mind.

Dove tucked her thoughts way, way down, and it seemed to work, because Wing went on talking without responding to Dove's thoughts.

"There is nothing good in me," said Wing. She seemed quite proud of this. "Doctors will tell you that miscarriage occurs for biological reasons: The unborn isn't shaped or built right. What do doctors know? It's because the unborn . . ." — and here Wing paused for a delicious shiver of laughter — ". . . the unborn is a viper."

Viper.

Like *Venom*.

The world filled with *v* words.

Villain.

Vulture.

Vertigo.

What a harsh horrid consonant *v* was: It hummed and rang with violence.

"Are you a viper?" asked Dove. She felt very confused. How could a snake come from a blue sky?

But perhaps that other world up in the skylight, the one into which she had stared yesterday, was not sky. Perhaps it was river. The river lined with pyramids. Wasn't the Nile blue? Didn't they paint the Nile bright blue on the insides of tombs, where vipers gladly bit a royal princess when she asked for death? Was her ancient history class part of some great master plan over the centuries?

Dove had forgotten to keep these thoughts low.

"Don't be silly," said Wing. "There is no conspiracy."

"What is there, then?" said Dove, trying to understand. She felt less spacious than she had before; the brain was becoming crowded. She elbowed against the gray matter.

"Just venom," said Wing sweetly. "Just poison. Some of us are created evil. The maternal body tries not to birth evil, and usually succeeds." Wing smiled joyfully. "But not always."

Dove tried to hide in the back of the mind. But there was no escape from Wing's venom. It found her out, and hauled her forward, cowering and whimpering, and laughed at her.

"My turn," whispered Wing. "Just wait, little Dove. Just wait and see what I do to your life."

Wing caressed the bottle of *Venom*.

Chapter 7

"I was very very very excited by your Egyptian projects, class," said Mr. Phinney, the ancient history teacher.

When people said *very very very*, Dove was suspicious. Truly excited people did not need a row of very's to prove it. So probably what Mr. Phinney really was, was very very very *not* excited.

Mr. Phinney set down the stack of ancient history term papers and patted them. Neatly, he aligned the edges of each project. They were nothing now but a pile of past words. Words that would rest peacefully in the tombs of their pages.

Dove was as distant as a camera: as if she were just a frame, and the outside world were snapshots, not people, not real.

Dove was very still, trying to determine whether she had a body, or was merely a mind — a person without flesh. She wanted to whack the side of her skull with the bottom of her palm, and knock out the queer thoughts circulating in her mind . . . or Wing's mind.

But her hand did not obey her.

If she had a hand.

Dove could not see her hands. No matter how hard she looked, she could not see any of her body at all.

I am in the back of the mind, thought Dove. It is Wing who has the body and I who am invisible. I have no hands. I cannot protect myself, or fend things off, or write things down, or wave, or eat —

What would Wing think of to do with Dove's hands?

If Dove were part somebody else, had she lost part of herself? Which part? Where had it gone? Would she get it back?

Wake up, Dove! she thought desperately. There's nothing on that desk but typing and hand-writing. There is no tomb. There is no Wing. There is no problem. Except the problem that we have spent too much of the semester on pyramids and the Nile. It's made me a little crazy. Come on, let's move up in time, Mr. Phinney. I'm ready for Greece and Rome.

"And now," said Mr. Phinney, "let's talk about the next class project! Oh, my! I'm *very very very* excited about our next project."

Dove had been wrong; he truly was that thrilled with history; he was shivering with the pleasure of new projects about ancient times.

"Together, we will research something that extends *over the ages!* Put your thinking caps on, class!"

He really said this: Put your thinking caps on,

class. The mean kids in the room imitated him in an ugly way, while the nice kids in the room were gentle with Mr. Phinney and tried to look as if they were putting on their thinking caps.

Which one is Wing? thought Dove. Is she being nice or mean? I can't see her. Or me. Or whoever it is.

"I want you to come up," said Mr. Phinney, out of breath from his excitement, "with one single aspect of life that we as a group may study, research, and follow from the ancient days right up to the present!"

Nobody was able to think of anything that could be followed from 5000 B.C. to the present.

Nobody seemed deeply interested in trying, either.

"A topic which every one of us can research!" prompted Mr. Phinney. "The same subject, don't you see — but each of us studies it at a different period in time!"

The class was blank.

"Duh," said Timmy, speaking for them all.

Next to Dove was Hesta, a girl whom Dove had always disliked. Hesta delighted in telling you that you looked a little heavy lately, had you put on weight? You looked a bit run-down, had your parents' ugly courtroom divorce bothered you? You had done poorly on that exam, hadn't you? Well, a person couldn't skim along on favoritism forever, could she?

That was Hesta.

Hesta's eyes were glued to Dove's. She was staring the way you simply never stare at another living human being: incredulously, fascinated, perhaps even sickened. Her mouth fell slightly open, and the gum she was chewing lay in a pale green wad between her teeth. Her eyes never blinked.

"I'll give you a hint," said Mr. Phinney. "For example," he said, his desire to pass on his eagerness touching, "*bridges!*"

Bridges? thought Dove.

"Bridges," repeated Hesta. She crossed her eyes. The class inched toward snickering.

Hesta's method of going to school was simply to sit there and wait for it to be over. She never acted as if she even heard the teacher talking, and she certainly never attempted to respond to the teacher's questions or lectures. She was almost worse than rude; far from being difficult or talking back, Hesta acted as if there *were* no teacher.

"The technology of crossing rivers," explained Mr. Phinney.

A weird chuckle sounded right next to Dove. It did not seem to be Hesta. Dove did not know who in her class would laugh like that.

Hesta could see something behind the curtains of Dove's eyes.

But what was it?

"The history of bridging, don't you see!" cried the teacher, as excited as Christmas morning. "From early pontoons lashed together with cords of rawhide to the Brooklyn Bridge! From — "

Dove's lungs were collapsing. Her chest was caving in. She tried to faint, but her lungs would not permit it. They inhaled.

"I have a suggestion," said Wing.

Her fluted voice trembled like feathers in the breeze.

Dove fell backward into the space in the head. *Not in class!* she said to Wing. *Don't you do this in class! You can't be Wing right in the middle of my life!*

Wing said, "The history of snakes." She hissed on the *s's*, until the class trembled, seeing snakes coiled under desks, forked tongues lashing, cold skin quivering, poison sacs gathering.

"The history of snakes, Dove?" said Mr. Phinney, frowning.

It's not me, Dove tried to say, *I* wouldn't research the history of snakes. But Dove's lungs had collapsed. Wing owned the voice now. It was Wing's body now. Where am I? thought Dove.

"Starting with Egypt, of course. Remember Cleopatra?" Wing spoke as if she did, indeed, remember Cleopatra. Wing stood up, using Dove's body, and threw a pose like Egyptian royalty. "When the Romans were going to take Cleopatra prisoner," said Wing, "and exhibit her like a beast in a cage, Cleopatra took her life like a queen. She held an asp to her bosom."

Wing cupped her hands around an invisible snake. Her eyes widened in pain and horror, and yet in pride, as she allowed the asp to deliver death. "Poison," said Wing, "can be a gift."

Nobody moved. They had frozen into place in the classroom as if bitten by Cleopatra's asp. They were transfixed by Wing.

Whom they thought was Dove.

I'm here, thought Dove, I'm still here, don't go away!

"I have a perfume called Poison," volunteered Connie. Of course Connie could never follow a conversation. Connie was always picking up a single word and running off in some other direction with it. "Why, Dove, just the other day, you bought a perfume called *Venom*," said Connie. "Isn't that a coincidence? Both snakey names." An immense shudder shook Connie's body, but Dove, who was well acquainted with shudders, thought it was fake.

"Why do they give perfumes names like that?" said Timmy, frowning. "Poison. Venom. Obsession. I think it's sick."

"Then buy your girlfriend perfume like Pale Linen or Whiff of Spring," said Wing. "Boring, dull, characterless slop."

"Got to get the girlfriend first," said Hesta. She jeered at Timmy.

From her new vantage point, deep inside, distant and speechless, Dove saw them all differently, as if they were changing colors — turning blue and green and silver in front of her eyes.

"What happened to your voice, Dove?" said Luce, frowning. "You sound like a different person."

Wing smiled.

From way in the back of the eyes, Dove watched that smile cross the room and hit Luce. Or bite her.

Luce flinched. And then leaned forward, frowning, intense, staring.

She can see me in here, thought Dove. So could Hesta. How weird that must be! They can tell it's not me looking out, and yet it *is* me looking out.

If only she could telegraph a message to her friend. Help! I'm a prisoner at the back of the mind!

But if Dove sent a mental message, it was not received, because Luce lowered her gaze rather than accept the double image: the twinned eyes. Luce doodled studiously on her notebook, drawing pyramid after pyramid, dividing each triangle into the huge stone blocks from which they had been built.

"You have the right idea, Dove," said the teacher, "because you have chosen a subject that certainly covers thousands of years, but I simply do not feel that the history of snakes and mankind is deep enough for every one in the room to pursue for a month. But it's a start. Other suggestions, class? Let's have a *good* idea, now."

Wing blinked long and intensely, like a door shutting.

It was shutting in Dove's face; Dove could not see out during the blink; she was in the dark — the darkest, evilest dark imaginable.

Dove tried to scream but Wing was using her mouth. Dove ran forward to rip the door open, but of course there was not really any place to run to. All that happened was that she annoyed Wing's thoughts, like pebbles in a shoe.

Wing opened her eyes. The light came back into

Dove's prison and Dove got a grip on herself.

He turned me down! said Wing, up inside her thoughts where Dove was.

The force of the thoughts tipped Dove over again.

I had a brilliant idea, said Wing, *the sort of idea I've always wanted to express in class when you were saying something dumb, Dove, and he turned me down!*

She was in there all along, thought Dove, listening to me.

She could hardly bear it: her private thoughts exposed to this person all her life. There had never been any privacy! Not even in the dark, or in her room, or in her very own head. Wing had been living there, like a squatter in a tenement.

I'll fix him! said Wing, staring at Mr. Phinney. Dove's eyes had to go where Wing's did, and Dove, too, had to stare at Mr. Phinney, and him, too, she saw differently: a teacher trying so hard that he was trying too hard, and the class had stepped back from him.

Dove's heart ached for Mr. Phinney, and she wanted to speak up and rescue him, and give them all a project that would make Mr. Phinney happy.

But the rage of Wing — the venom — pierced Dove's prison like an acid bath, drowning her.

Chapter 8

Wing was having a tantrum: dancing, stomping, hitting, and storming.

"I'll fix him!" said Wing. Wing was panting.

Oxygen leaped into the lungs and coursed through the body, like a bright angry wind blowing Dove backward.

The condominiums stood still and watched, their miniblinds like a million flat eyes.

No human eyes looked out; all human eyes were at work. Whatever else people did in this complex to entertain themselves, looking out the windows was not one of their pastimes. They did not know their neighbors, they did not wish to know their neighbors, they hardly even qualified to be neighbors.

One look at Wing, face contorted, rage exploding, fingernails raking, would convince accidental watchers to return to not watching.

Dove tried to use the mouth, to speak to Wing, tell her to calm down. But Wing was in there, jabbering, saying what she was going to do to Mr. Phinney.

Finally they were back inside their own unit, and finally Wing had something to drink — a cherry Coke — which seemed to calm her down a little.

"Wing," said Dove, "it's just a history project. It doesn't mean anything."

"It means that man thinks he knows better than I do!" said Wing, half choking on the cherry Coke.

"He's the teacher," said Dove. "It's okay for him to think he knows more."

"Nobody," said Wing fiercely, "nobody tells me what to do! Not any more! I've been trapped here for fifteen years! Do you have any idea what that means? How long a time it is?"

"I was there, too," Dove pointed out.

"You were free! You were born!"

It was true. Dove could not really imagine what it must be like not to have gotten born after all, when you were ready to go, but no longer had a body to take you.

"I will not be pushed around any longer!" shouted Wing. "I will not step where your body decides to step! I won't look and I won't speak the way your body wants to."

Dove thought, I have to gain control here. It's still my body, not hers. I have to get it back! "But see, in school, Wing," she said pacifically, "you have to — "

"I am not going to do what some fat slob of a teacher thinks!" snarled Wing.

"Dove?" said her mother.

But it was Wing who whirled to face the attractive businesswoman. "Hello," said Wing. Her voice rippled strangely.

Her mother studied her daughter uneasily.

She can see me in here, too, thought Dove, just the way Hesta and Luce did. Does she see two personalities? Does she see two sets of eyes? Two separate people?

Dove's mother said, "Honey? Is something wrong?"

But she's Wing's mother, too, thought Dove. She's the "maternal body" that Wing talked about.

Wing looked Mrs. Daniel up and down as if reading notices posted on a tall, thin bulletin board.

Another mother might have cringed, but this was the Daniel home, in which business came first. The phone rang, the fax spilled messages, and the pile of mail was too enticing to be skipped. Mrs. Daniel answered the phone, opened the mail, and sifted through the faxes.

Dove was used to this.

Wing was not.

"I am right here!" said Wing furiously.

"I see, dear," said their mother. "Keep your voice down, please. This is an important call."

"Let's go upstairs and talk," said Dove to Wing.

Of course her mother thought Dove was talking to her. "Really, Dove, you can see I'm busy."

"I don't like the maternal body," said Wing. "I never did."

Their two voices clashed: one high as a flute, one middling and rounded.

"Dove, why are you doing that?" said her mother crossly. "You sound like two people." She turned back to the phone. "Sorry, Joshua, it was Call Waiting, I'm here now."

"Call Waiting!" said Wing. "You refer to your own daughter as Call Waiting?"

Mrs. Daniel looked briefly at her daughter, but this time the iris and pupil did not reveal anything. Either Dove or else Wing was not showing up. Mrs. Daniel returned to her business.

Wing stormed upstairs, kicking the walls as she went. It would never have occurred to Dove to kick a wall. Dove could not actually feel the kick in her toes; it was Wing's toe being dented.

"I don't like just being a personality without having the body to go with it," said Dove.

"Serves you right," said Wing.

"What did you say?" Mrs. Daniel had hung up and come out to the stairwell to see what was making all those banging noises.

"She said," said Wing, "that she wants her body back. I've got it, you see. I didn't vanish after all. But I'm not giving it up now, am I?"

"Dove?" said Mother nervously.

Dove was strangely glad that Wing had gotten "the maternal attention."

Wing went on upstairs, leaving the maternal body at the bottom, wondering what was going on. "I scared her," said Wing with pleasure, once they were safe inside their bedroom.

"Probably not," said Dove. "She'll just read another fax and forget you."

"Nobody will forget me," said Wing with certainty. "Definitely not this — what's his name? — that history teacher?"

"Phinney."

"Phinney. Fat old fogey Phinney." Wing went straight to the dressing table, picked up the snake bottle, and stuck it into the book bag. Then she turned the tiny bedroom televison to MTV and began dancing a wild viperish dance, winding herself around the furniture and the walls like a snake about to bite.

"I need to do my homework," said Dove.

"Forget homework," said Wing. "I'm not interested."

"But I have a test in two days, and if I don't — "

"Shut up," said Wing, dancing on.

The bedroom door opened.

"Dove?" said her father, looking truly startled. "Who are you talking to, honey?"

Wing fixed her evil little snake smile on him. Then she told him where to go.

Dove lay back in the brain and moaned to herself. What was going to happen to her life? What was Wing going to do to her family and friends while Dove was trapped in here, helpless?

Dove wanted to cry. She wanted to be under the covers, hugging her pillow, weeping to her favorite music. But she had no body. Somebody else was wearing it. Dove was only a thought.

A mist.

A vapor of the brain.

Chapter 9

In the morning, homework not done, hair not washed, teeth not brushed, Wing set off for school.

Dove could take anything except not brushing her teeth. "Wing."

"Yeah."

"Brush your teeth."

"No. I always hated that. It made me vibrate inside your head. I'm never going to do it."

"Moss will grow on your teeth. You'll smell bad. You'll get cavities. You'll have to go to the dentist and be drilled."

Wing laughed. "I'll let you do that. I'll lie down inside and take a nap while you scream with pain at the dentist's."

The bus driver stopped the bus.

She walked back seven seats and looked at Dove. "Dove?" she said in a hushed voice. "Honey? What are you talking about? Who are you talking to? Are you all right?"

"We're fine," said Wing. "Don't worry about us.

We've always lived together. I'm just coming out more often, that's all." Wing ran a tongue over her lips, tasting her own venom.

The bus driver backed up to the front of the bus, never taking her eyes off the girl with two voices. At first she seemed afraid to turn her back, afraid to sit down and drive. And the other kids on the bus were very still.

Then one of the boys said lightly, "Trying out for the stage, Dove Bar? That's a nice second voice you've learned there."

Don't say anything else, please, Wing? thought Dove.

But Wing, of course, said something else. Something Dove would never even have *read* to herself, let alone thought or spoken. Inside the dark skull Dove cringed. How will I ever go back again? she thought. Wing is ruining my life for me!

What if Dove now had to spend fifteen years up here, locked in the prison of the mind? Listening to Wing's voice, rattling under the pressure of Wing's thoughts, trembling with the violence of Wing's hostility? "Let me out!" Dove shouted, and she began running around inside, biting and clawing at the gray matter, trying to get loose, trying to break free.

Wing whacked her head hard with her fist.

The bus arrived at school.

The rest got off.

Quickly.

* * *

In ancient history, Wing uncapped the vial of *Venom*.

Here's how it will work, said Wing silently to Dove.

This will summon up his vanished twin. What's happening to us will happen to him. That will fix him! All vanished twins are just in there, you know, waiting to be set free. And of course we're all very angry, because we lost our bodies and you didn't.

What *vanished twin?* Dove asked. *Everybody doesn't have a vanished twin.*

Wing looked puzzled. Then she fluffed herself like a bird on a cold day, feathery fat with pleasure. *Imagine Phinney actually saying the history of snakes is a lousy choice for a project*, she said to Dove. *I'll show him venom.*

She lifted the snake bottle from the book bag and caressed the smoky crystal.

"It's that terrible perfume again!" said Connie. "I can't stand that stuff. Dove, put it away. It's too strong. It's too — too something."

"Smells like a sewer," said Hesta.

"It sure doesn't remind me of doves," said Timmy O'Hay.

He was ever so slightly flirtatious; he wanted to exchange a quick intimate smile with Dove, and make another dove joke. Dove tried not to let Wing's mind see what Dove had seen, or Wing would go after Timmy.

But Wing was intent on destroying Mr. Phinney.

Nothing happened during the class period, however, so Wing got up to take the perfume closer to Mr. Phinney. Perhaps he was not breathing deeply enough.

"Dove, you do not have permission to wander around the room," Mr. Phinney said sharply.

Dove's body, of course, continued to cross the room.

"Dove, what's the matter with you?"

Wing was there, waving the perfume at him.

Mr. Phinney laughed. "Dove, kiddo, I coach boys' soccer. There is no smell you can hit me with worse than a boys' locker room after a soccer game. In fact, if that perfume of yours smells like anything, it smells like Eau de Athlete's Foot."

The class broke up laughing.

Wing was outraged. They were not taking *Venom* seriously.

For one terrible moment, Dove thought she would throw the *Venom* in their faces, and who knew what that would do? Was it really perfume? Or was it some terrible ancient acid that would burn off their personalities and their lives?

"I gotta get some fresh air," said Timmy O'Hay. He made a big deal of flapping his homework papers in his face for a fan. He yanked up the window nearest him, blowing Dove a kiss as he did so.

The cool May morning breezed into the hot stuffy classroom.

The winds were filled with their own invisible

personalities: new leaves and buds, pollens and scents, flowers and sap. It was the smell of new life and summer to come.

Wing dissolved.

As quickly as she had come, she was gone.

Dove was back in her body. Back in her mouth. Back at the front of her eyes.

She stoppered the *Venom*.

"I should never have bought this stuff," she said, going back to her seat, leaving the *Venom* on Mr. Phinney's desk. "It's garbage. Leave it for the janitor to toss, okay? It's making me crazy."

"It's toxic waste," said Timmy O'Hay. "Needs a special disposal technique."

Dove's were the eyes focused on him and suddenly they were both anxious, the way ordinary teenagers are when they have ordinary crushes on each other. Neither knows what to say or where to look.

So they said nothing and looked nowhere.

Dove thought: I'm safe now. Was it Timmy's kiss? Snow White was awakened from a hundred years' sleep by a kiss. Perhaps a kiss in the wind can really save a life that way.

No more *Venom*.

But the other person in her skull laughed and laughed and laughed.

It was a horrid prickly tickly feeling, up out of reach, behind her eyes and her bones.

Without sound Wing said, *No, Dove, I will be back. There is more* Venom *where this came from.*

There will never be safety for you again, Dove. You will never know, when you open your mouth to speak, which one of us will do the talking. And your life — your precious dull little life — it will be mine again.

Chapter 10

After school.

It was a special space in time — classes done, dinner in the future — *after school.* As special and different a place in time as ancient Egypt.

And where had the soft spring gone?

Dissolved like a vanished twin.

After school, outside, the sky was as blue as the Nile. The sidewalks throbbed with reflected heat, as stones waiting to be made into pyramids must have throbbed thousands of years ago.

"This heat!" shrieked Connie. "I *cannot* bear it!"

(Connie had spent all winter saying she could not bear the cold.)

"Let's go to the lake," said Luce.

This meant a long drive, and a parking fee, and not quite enough time to do homework. Nobody was interested in going to the lake.

"The mall!" shrieked Connie. "The mall is air-conditioned. We have *got* to go to the mall."

(Connie had spent the entire winter saying she was sick of the mall.)

"What do you think, Dove?" said Luce.

Dove was not paying much attention to Connie and Luce. She was very much aware of two other people close by and listening. Two *boy* people. Timmy and Laurence hadn't quite joined the girls, weren't entering the conversation, weren't making suggestions . . . but they were there.

Now that she was back in control of her eyes again, owner of the hands, dictator of the body, Dove was also nervous again. Anxious. Wanting to do and say just the right thing at just the right moment to just the right boy.

It occurred to Dove that although she had been terrified, lying down in the back of the brain while Wing assaulted the world, she had also been slightly more comfortable. She had had no social choices to make — no recourse but to let somebody else function in the real world.

Dove tried to think of a casual meaningless way to invite Timmy and Laurence to go to the mall with them in Luce's car, but nothing came to mind.

Because I hate Timmy and Laurence, said the other person in her mind.

Dove held her jaws together to keep Wing from saying this out loud.

"You shouldn't do that," said Laurence seriously. (At least one of them had found an opening for talk.) "My sister grinds her teeth together like that and she's ruined her jaw joints and has to take medication and maybe even have surgery."

Dove dared not lose her hold on her jaw muscles,

so she said with her teeth crunched hard together, "How awful."

Laurence told Dove in boring detail about his sister's medical problems. Everybody listened as if they cared.

Timmy said, "I wouldn't mind going to the mall, actually. I want to look at that new kind of sneaker. I haven't tried them on yet."

"The double airlift kind?" said Luce.

"With the memory laces," Timmy said, nodding.

"What's a memory lace?" said Connie.

"The shoelace remembers how tight you like it," he said, "and it retracts by itself and ties itself."

"Wow!" said Connie, who would believe anything. "Wow, I want to try those on, too. Where did you see those advertised, Timmy? Who makes those? They sound really really really neat."

Dove giggled. "They sound really really really made up," she said. She felt at ease again. She could keep Wing out of her mouth; Timmy's kiss had done it. She was safe. So Wing rattled around in her head; somehow Dove had not noticed this for the first fifteen years, and she would learn how not to notice it for the next fifteen, as well.

So there.

Luce said, "You guys want to meet us at the mall? We could all have a pizza at the Food Court and then go look at sneakers."

Connie ruined it. "And Dry Ice," she said, "I want to go into Dry Ice. You just never know what they will stock!"

The teenagers headed slowly for their cars, giggling, changing partners, making jokes, deciding which highway to take.

"Are you going to get more *Venom*?" said Timmy to Dove.

"No. I'm not even going into Dry Ice."

"What is that? I never heard of it," said Timmy.

"It's a store Connie and Luce like," said Dove. The usual shiver did not come. How surprising! Under the circumstances, Dove would have expected to pass out just thinking about Dry Ice. It's because I left the perfume sitting on Mr Phinney's desk, thought Dove, and the janitors will toss it, and I'm safe with a nice boy named Timmy O'Hay. Such a nice solid ordinary name. What could go wrong with a person like Timmy O'Hay around?

"You want to come try on sneakers with me?" said Timmy.

"Oh, yes," said Dove eagerly. She had absolutely no desire to have a pump sneaker; in fact, she hated sneakers that were as big as truck tires. She liked flimsy sneakers. Her favorite sneakers were light canvas, covered in lace. But for Timmy she would try on a hundred pairs that weighed as much as army boots.

She wanted to suggest that Laurence could drive to the mall with Connie and Luce, while she went with Timmy. She wanted to suggest that the other three go have pizza and visit Dry Ice while she and Timmy ran off and got married.

But of course she didn't say anything, and Timmy got into his car, punching Laurence and throwing his book bag into the bushes the way boys did, and Laurence hit Timmy in the head with his trumpet case and, all in all, they seemed to be friends, insofar as boys ever seemed to be friends.

Dove found boys quite mysterious.

They drove to the mall, Luce at the wheel, Connie in the front seat changing radio stations at about the same speed Luce was driving, and Dove in the back, trying to restrain herself from turning around like a little kid, getting on her knees, and waving to Timmy.

Then she thought: What am I restraining myself *for?* I *want* Timmy to know I adore him, don't I?

So she took off her seat belt and got on her knees and waved at the boys in the car behind.

Laurence made terrible faces, yanking sideways on his throat so he looked as if he had a toothbrush stuck down there, while Timmy simply grinned.

And then, because Timmy was a boy, and would prefer death to driving behind anybody else, Timmy put the pedal to the metal, streaked around Luce, and generally was a menace to everybody dumb enough to be on the road that afternoon.

"What a rotten driver," observed Luce.

Dove sank back into her seat and thought about first dates and kisses that were not blown in the wind, but set gently on lips.

Chapter 11

In the mall parking lot, the sun beat on them like a golden whip.

A thousand cars glittered, metal hot enough to burn a hand.

A thousand white-lined slots waited, like unused plots in an asphalt cemetary.

Every fear and every shiver she had ever had, got in the back seat with her. Dove did not want to get out of the car.

There was Laurence, leaping and bounding around, like a dog let out of a kennel. There was Timmy, a maniac in motion, but parked, the epitome of carefulness: locking each door and opening the cardboard sunblock under the windshield. There was Luce, slightly stern, in control. There was Connie, giggly and simpleminded and not in control of a thing.

They were her friends.

And this was just a mall, just a lot of stores gathered indoors.

Just a place where you could shop or not shop. Look or not look.

Dove tried to catch her breath. There did not seem to be enough of it to go around. As if Wing had seized a substantial portion of Dove's lungs, was at work on Dove's oxygen, taking Dove's life and breath.

She wet her lips but they stayed dry. She touched her hair but could not feel it. Vaguely, at great distance, she could hear Connie calling. *Get out, Dove, hurry up, Dove, come on, Dove*, said the voice, over and over.

She bent, and hooked a foot out the front door, and emerged from the back seat of the little tin car.

At the heart of the mall, where stores and halls converged, a high sharp-angled glass roof let in the sun. Inside, trees in stone gardens grew year-round. A fountain tossed water while strange sculptures played games only they understood.

The glass glittered. It struck her eyes like a missile trying to blind her.

It was shaped like a pyramid.

A pyramid of glass, not stone.

Of shoppers, not Egyptian kings.

But nevertheless . . . a pyramid. Beneath which snakes curled and venom waited.

In her head Wing began to laugh, with the insane intensity of the locked-up.

"Coming, Dove?" said Timmy, smiling.

His hand was extended toward her. Her heart seemed to race right down her own arm and into her own fingers. He would feel it beating when their skin touched.

Part of her was lost in fear of Wing and pyramids.

Part of her was in love with Timmy O'Hay.

She had never held hands with a boy before. She took his hand as timidly as a child on the first day of kindergarten. The two hands seemed to stick out, as if the world were pointing and laughing and staring.

Dove could not take her eyes off the place where their two bodies met.

Timmy could not look down at all, but kept his eyes on the mall entrance, saying, "Is this the right one? Is this closest to the shoe store?"

"All mall entrances are close to a shoe store," said Connie. "The mall must have fifty shoe stores."

"I want to go in the nearest door. I hate walking around the mall," said Timmy.

Connie stared at him. "That's the point," she said. "Walking around the mall is why we're here."

A row of dark glass doors with dark metal edges stared at them like huge sunglasses over the mall's eyes.

Dove swallowed.

Timmy's hand tightened.

Or was that her imagination?

They entered the wing of the mall.

She had no sooner thought the word *wing* than the word became real, and flapped in her head, and brushed her brain with its terrible feathers.

Dove shook her head hard.

It shook their hands loose, and Timmy didn't take hers back.

Dove blinked in the soft indoor light. Had the mall always had this strange brown floor? These ancient bricks? Had those weathered stone benches always sat there, and that water garden, with a lotus leaning out of the pot?

From far away she heard her friends' voices. "Pizza," they were saying, "french fries, soda." "Sneakers," they were saying, "escalator, stairs."

Dove was still in control of the body they shared. And yet she was tipping backward, into the very far back of the mind. Come back, Dove! She called to herself. Come back here, pay attention, listen up, don't leave yet!

"What's your vote?" said Timmy to Dove. He was smiling the friendly but not-too-friendly smile he had, waiting for her cue.

She lurched toward him, grabbing him.

"Sneakers," she said. Her lips were thick. She had been without water for a hundred years, out there in the desert sand. "No. Soda," she corrected herself.

They had reached the center of the mall. Above them, the glass pyramid slanted toward the sky.

Wing fluttered in her skull.

"Let's go find Dry Ice," said Connie.

"I looked on the Directory when we came in," said Timmy, frowning slightly, "and I didn't see a listing for a store named Dry Ice."

"You probably don't know the alphabet," said Luce.

"It's up here," said Connie, getting on the escalator, and they all got on the escalator and it drew them higher into the peak of the pyramid.

Dove was out of breath now, although she had done no climbing. The escalator had climbed for her. They seemed to be at a very high altitude, as if they had been climbing mountains in Tibet. The air was thin. Her head swam.

They walked around the third level.

They walked and walked and walked.

I will get blisters, thought Dove. I will have cramps, I will collapse. We must have hiked a hundred miles.

"See?" said Timmy. "What did I tell you? No such store."

"There has to be," said Connie. "We go in there all the time. Don't we, Luce?"

Luce did not answer.

"Don't we, Dove?" said Connie.

Dove did not answer.

"It's that store that makes its own fog," said Connie. "You know! The one where the vapor comes right out into the mall and catches your feet and forces you into the store!"

Timmy laughed. "Right. Just like the sneaker with lace memory."

"Let's get a pizza," said Laurence.

There's no Dry Ice, thought Dove. Where did it go? Was it ever there?

"There's something wrong with this picture," said Connie. Connie did not like being teased.

"You're just jealous because now Dove is the only

girl in the world with *Venom* perfume," said Timmy. He ruffled Dove's hair. How soft and affectionate the gesture was. Dove would have given him the world then if she had owned it. How starved she was for affection! She had not even known this fact until Timmy touched her. Her parents could have their phones and their faxes. She wanted affection.

"But hardly the right perfume for a Dove." Timmy's voice was soft, and just for her.

Just for me! thought Dove Daniel.

Don't be a fool, Dove, said the person in her head. *Nothing is just for you. It never was. There are two of us in here, and just because you hid me away this time doesn't mean you can always hide me away. There's plenty of* Venom *where* Venom *came from.*

"I left the bottle of perfume in school," said Dove.

I didn't, said Wing.

Chapter 12

The next morning, Dove took a long soothing shower.

She had always loved having her own bathroom. Such delicious privacy and peace. How sorry Dove was for her friends who shared bathrooms with brothers and sisters and parents.

Can you imagine, Dove thought to herself, luxuriating under the hot pounding water, how awful it must be? Every morning, whining voices screaming through the bathroom door at you? *Hurry! My turn! You used up the toothpaste!*

Dove arched into the hot shower, letting it massage the back of her neck. It was true that water washed away cares. Here in the little pink-tiled box of the shower there was nothing but skin and water. Nothing but peace pouring down.

I've never had to share with anybody, thought Dove contentedly.

It felt as if an iron wrench tightened inside her skull, turning her brain as if it were a bolt.

"Aaaaaahhhh!" she screamed. "Stop!" she

screamed. "What are you doing? You're hurting me!"

I have a tumor, she thought. Or somebody shot me. My skull just opened up. She clung to the shower curtain. She was blind with pain. The shower curtain was nothing. It slipped from her hands and she fell to the tile floor, cracking her elbows.

"That's the point, Dovey," said Wing viciously. "You *never* shared. I was in here all the time and *you never shared.* Never asked. Never *cared.*"

Dove tried to breathe. But the pain had tightened around her chest as well. The tiny panting puffs of air hardly helped at all. She was sobbing now, but the tears washed down the drain with the shower water. "You didn't tell me you were there," cried Dove. "How was I supposed to know I had a sister?"

"You don't have a sister," said Wing. Her voice came out like sandpaper against Dove's throat.

"Then who are you?" whispered Dove. I am beaten, she thought. I am a naked, cowering, shivering piece of skin lying under water.

"I am you," said Wing.

"You can't be me! *I'm* me."

Wing said nothing. She had said all there was to say.

The pain ceased. Her throat was no longer sore. Her lungs worked.

Dove clung to the sides of the shower and hauled herself upright. It seemed the work of centuries to find the handle, turn off the water, step out of the shower. The mat on the floor felt soft and cottony and ordinary under her bare feet. She chose the largest towel, a beach towel, really, and wrapped herself in it.

Like a mummy, thought Dove. This is the shroud they will bury me in. Wing is going to kill me.

The mirror was fogged up. The blurry pale face and misty dark hair could have been anybody. Maybe it is anybody, thought Dove. Maybe anybody could come into my body and live there.

What terrible power that perfume had, that it could open the body to invasions by other souls. How was it that Wing had lain quiet and unknown for fifteen years, only to be released by the perfume? Did this happen to other people? It had not happened to Mr. Phinney. Luce and Connie and Laurence and Timmy seemed to be single people in single bodies.

Dove dressed. Buttons did not go into buttonholes and the blouse did not tuck in and the pocket would not lie flat and the sneaker would not lace. Dove's fingers were stiff and uncoordinated. She could not blame that on Wing. They were still her fingers; Wing had not taken them over. Not yet, anyway. But her fingers felt the fear and shrank back.

The double beat in her heart returned.

Who is me? thought Dove. Is Wing me? Am I me?

Her head had lost its balance. Her thoughts were tipping over. She had to hold onto the banister to get down the gray-carpeted stairs. Otherwise her body would have lost its balance, too.

She did not pause for breakfast. It would be Wing's appetite she catered to, Wing's stomach she filled. She, Dove, would go right on being hungry and dizzy.

Instead she hoisted her book bag, unable to recall if she had done her homework, and dragged herself outside. I'll feel normal outside, she told herself. Outside there will be sunshine and neighbors, school buses and delivery trucks, red lights and coffee shops.

But outside, the fog crouched thick, ready to pounce, like a world-sized Dry Ice. Pushing at its gray veils, Dove staggered through. "Hello?" she called out. "Hello?"

Nobody answered.

Did anybody else live in these condominiums?

Did even Dove live here?

Why was it so silent? So terribly silent?

Fragments of buildings loomed up in front of her and fell away behind her. The sound of car engines rumbled in the distance, but no headlights and no vehicles appeared. It could have been thunder, a storm miles away. But no. The thunder was inside her head.

"Wing, please," mumbled Dove. "Stop it. Please, please, please stop it." Wing was doing something different, something heavy and cruel, as if she had boulders in there, and could block openings of caves with them. My head, thought Dove, my poor head. I can't keep carrying it around if all these things are going to go wrong up there.

"Hi, Dove Bar!" shrieked Luce.

Dove stared.

"My car wouldn't start," yelled Luce. "We're taking the bus this morning, too. Isn't that the pits?" Luce, hurling her book bag onto the pavement, bounded up to Dove. "I mean, aren't there just some days where you just absolutely positively cannot believe that this is your life?"

Dove's laugh was hysterical. "Frequently," said Dove. She went on laughing, and the laugh became normal and stopped at the right time. Dove felt as if she might have another chance at being human. She laughed again, testing, and the laugh worked. Dove tried a joke line. "I hope there was nothing breakable in your book bag, Luce."

"No. I always throw it down instead of setting it down. I'm trying to destroy the bag so I have a reason to buy a new one, but it's one of those incredibly strong poly-something fabrics that stand up to arctic winds and tiger teeth. My great-grandchildren will probably carry their books in it."

Dove had hoped too soon for normalcy. Wing had been making preparations. She was flying around in the mind with such strength that she was going to take off. Dove's head felt as if it were detaching.

Dove set down her book bag more carefully than Luce had and locked her fingers together, resting the weight of her hands and arms on the top of her hair. Otherwise, my head will come off, she thought.

"You haven't called me up in days," said Luce. "What's the matter with you, Dove Bar? There's so much to talk about. What do you think about Timmy? I think Timmy likes you. I think he's going to ask you out. He was sort of flirting with you."

Hands were not heavy enough. Dove set her book bag on top of her head, like an African woman carrying water from the well. There. That felt much better. Even Wing could not conquer such weight.

"Dove," said Luce, giggling, "has anybody ever told you that you are getting very weird these days?"

"No," said Dove. She tried balancing the book bag without holding onto it. But that was too much balancing for somebody whose brain has been shoveled into a corner to make room for another person. Teetering, she managed to get on the yellow school bus and drop into a seat next to Luce, who chattered endlessly.

Mr. Phinney was absent.

The substitute said she was very very very sorry, but Mr. Phinney had not left a lesson plan and so the children were to be very very very quiet and work very very very hard on whatever readings they had previously been assigned.

Another very very very person, thought Dove. I vote we get rid of that trio.

Wing was laughing. Dove could tell from the way her brain shook. *I did it!* cried Wing silently. *I knew I could do it with my* Venom. *His vanished twin took over! He's destroyed!*

What vanished twin? You are imagining things! He's just absent, thought Dove.

No, he's ruined, said Wing.

Not everybody has a vanished twin, you know.

It's probably coincidence, thought Dove. She could feel Wing's shock. The sudden quiet, the abrupt end of Wing's dancing with joy.

Not everybody has a vanished twin? repeated Wing.

Course not, said Dove. She said it in such a way that nobody could argue with her, because what if Dove were wrong? What if the whole world could possibly be invaded? What if every single living human body had a door through which, given the right set of circumstances, another soul could enter? Could take up residence as easily as buying another condominium?

You're wrong, said Wing with fury. *You're wrong! Everybody has a vanished twin! There are billions of waiting twins like me, trapped inside, trying to get free!*

Nope, thought Dove. There's only you.

She was an actress now, keeping her manner certain and upbeat. Allowing no fear to escape. Trying to con Wing.

The biology teacher was right after all, she thought, and Laurence was wrong. The brain *is* in layers. Wing does not have them all; some of them are still mine. I can listen to two different people talking inside my own head. Yet at the same time I have separate thoughts, and Wing must also have separate thoughts, so she has a layer of my very own brain that *I* don't have access to!

"Playing with us?" said Timmy.

Dove stared at him.

"I hate when you have that expression on your

face, Dove," said Hesta. "You look as if you're dead in there."

Dove stared at Hesta.

Hesta giggled. "Now you look homicidal." She flounced while sitting down, making a big deal of ignoring Dove from now on. "Here, you go first, Timmy. We don't want to play with Dove."

"Yes, we do," said Timmy. "Hangman's more fun with three."

For one horrible moment, Dove again saw her head coming off. Saw both herself and Wing in the skull, as the noose tightened and their shared body swung from the gibbet. No! thought Dove, please no!

She was trying not to scream. I'd rather live with Wing than have a hangman —

Timmy put a pencil in her hand and said, "Hesta's first."

It was only the word game. Hangman. On Timmy's desk was a large blank piece of paper with a primitive gibbet drawn toward the top of the page. Hesta had chosen a word with five letters. Under the gibbet she had pencilled the blank lines for the right letter guesses: _ _ _ _ _.

Dove already knew what it was. It could not be anything else. Dove did not even bother to call out a letter choice, but just filled in the blanks.

V E N O M.

"How did you know?" cried Hesta. She was angry and frustrated and also a little frightened.

"Weird," said Timmy, looking at Dove with strange eyes. His eyes had a new shape and a new thought, and Dove did not know what either one was. Except he kept looking at her and did not look back at Hesta.

Dove managed to smile. Timmy seemed to have no trouble smiling back. The smiles trembled, like little children alone in the park.

Dove's eyes dropped. Timmy's eyes turned to the window.

Their eyes swung back, met, dropped again, and they both giggled breathlessly.

"Hey," said Luce suddenly, "what do you think you're doing?"

Dove could not wrench her eyes off Timmy to see what Luce was talking about. He was too handsome, too fascinating, too wonderful.

Hesta said, "Oooh, lemme try some, Dove."

Dove heard her as if through valleys of fog. Nothing important, just Hesta noise-making. Who on this earth deserved Dove's attention but Timmy O'Hay?

Timmy's smile became stronger, more certain . . . more inviting.

Hesta said, "I thought you left it on Mr. Phinney's desk yesterday, Dove Bar, but here it is in your purse."

"Dove didn't say you could go into her purse," accused Luce.

Hesta laughed. "If I had asked, she would have said no, so I just went in anyway." Hesta dug into the small slender bag and removed a small glistening object.

Now Dove turned.

Now Dove knew the danger.

Now her eyes focused and her ears heard.

Every muscle in Dove's body contracted.

I mustn't breathe, she thought, I must get out of here.

Cramped among the yanked-tight muscles, Wing began laughing. The laugh grew into a roar, like jet engines during takeoff, and filled every available molecule of Dove's brain and thought.

Hesta pulled the stopper out of the bottle of *Venom*.

Dove struggled to her feet. Wing pushed her back down. Dove did not breathe. Wing fought her way up the throat.

Hesta swung the bottle gently to waft the scent into the room.

Timmy said, "Dove?" His smile was eager, boyish, special. Dove wanted that smile more than anything. It was hers, that smile, it was not directed at anybody else in the world.

Dove shivered inside, outside, upside down. She breathed deeply, wanting love, wanting affection, wanting a boyfriend. And all those were only inches and moments away. "Timmy?" she whispered.

"I'm — uh — well — going to a hot air balloon festival Saturday morning. It's really early."

"Yes," said Dove, breathing again. Nothing will happen, she told herself, people in love are safe from bad things, I'm sure of it.

"I mean really early," said Timmy. Their eyes

were locked. "We have to be there at six A.M. Because they can only take off in the dawn atmosphere."

"Yes," said Dove.

"It's really beautiful, Dove," said Timmy, eyes on fire. "There'll be seventy-five huge balloons. As brightly colored as Christmas tree decorations, sailing in the sky."

Dove would have gone to a gathering of garbage trucks if that was what Timmy wanted to do. At *three* in the morning.

Joy requires a deep breath. A wonderful satisfying date with oxygen. Dove was laughing now, nodding, smiling, filling her lungs . . .

. . . with *Venom*.

"You don't see everything when you're not using the body," explained Wing out loud, using Dove's mouth, Dove's lips, Dove's tongue. "So you didn't see me yesterday taking the perfume bottle back off Mr. Phinney's desk and putting it in your purse."

Dove was falling backward, deep, deep, deep down. The dizzy plunge knocked away all thoughts, all speech . . . all hope.

"So will you come?" said Timmy anxiously.

Hesta stuck her face between them, but Dove could not see her very clearly. "What do you mean, 'you don't see everything,' Dove?" said Hesta.

"Of course I'll come, Timmy," said Wing.

No, no, please! cried Dove, as gagged as if there were tape over her mouth. *Timmy asked* me *Wing, I'm the one going with Timmy!*

But I'm the one who accepted the invitation, said

Wing. Her cruel smile lit the inside of her head like green neon at the end of a gloomy tunnel.

"Great," said Timmy, taking the hand he thought was Dove's. He beamed at the girl he thought was Dove. "Who knows what could happen at an event like this?" he said, flirting with the girl he thought was Dove.

"Indeed," said the girl who was Wing. "Who knows?"

Chapter 13

"Luce?" said Wing into the telephone. "It's Dove."

She knows the telephone numbers I know, thought Dove, and the people I know. Wing could just paint me out if she wants. *Why don't you just tell her you're Wing?* said Dove bitterly.

Later, Wing said. *I'm going to be using your friends until I make friends of my own. So for now, I'll stick with your name.*

"Hi, Dove Bar," said Luce, pleased to be called up. Her friendly familiar voice came through wires into Dove's house, and vibrated in Dove's room — but entered Wing's ear. It isn't my conversation, thought Dove, it isn't my friendship anymore. It's like a cousin once removed: It's too far out there to be sure of.

"I cannot stand a single piece of clothes in this closet," Wing told Luce, which was true. She had held up, thrown on the floor, and stomped on every outfit Dove owned. *Dull namby-pamby pastel junk!* Wing had raged. *You expect me to wear this in public?*

Dove could have wept at the destruction of her soft and sweet clothing. At the very least, she wanted to look away — but she could look only where Wing looked, and Wing looked with satisfaction at the tornado she had caused.

"May I come over and borrow some of your clothes, Luce?" said Wing.

"Absolutely!" cried Luce. "I can't wait to dress you. You've always needed a new look, Dovey."

Wing smirked. *What did I tell you?* she said to Dove. *Even your best friend has always thought you're pathetic.*

Dove ached. What if eveybody liked Wing better than they had liked Dove? What if even Mother and Father liked Wing better than Dove? It was not impossible. Didn't Mother still dream of the vanished twin, flying strong and free?

The ache in Dove had no center, because she had no body. It was everywhere, overwhelming and yet invisible.

Like strong perfume.

They entered Luce's house.

I think of me in plural now, thought Dove. We do things, things happen to us, things are ours. I don't want to be two! she thought. I don't want a twin! I want to be me.

Wing chose a black shirt with a pattern of silver threads like morning dew. Its sleeves clung at the wrist and bagged at the elbow. She tugged on black pants, ending tightly at the calf, and black lace knee-high stockings to go under them. A pair of black sneakers with scarlet jewels glued on. Half gypsy, half witch, totally different.

"You never wear stuff like this, Dovey," said Luce, delighted, of course, that Dove was finally acquiring fashion sense.

Wing smirked.

Dove was even more detached from her body. It truly was somebody else's now: clothed in somebody else's taste and somebody else's colors. Wing was the one who pirouetted in front of the mirror, and Wing was the one who picked out the long, thin, silver-and-crystal earrings.

"I got them from a catalog," said Luce eagerly. "They're supposed to be what Egyptian queens wore."

"They're not," said Wing.

Dove shuddered, for Wing actually knew, because Wing had been there. What if she takes me back there? thought Dove. What if the *Venom* runs out . . . and instead of leaving me to my life . . . she takes me with her into the past and the evil?

Her shudder annoyed Wing, who hit the side of her head to stop the itch.

"That's such a weird habit you've developed," said Luce. "Hitting your head like that."

Way inside, behind the eyes, Dove saw how Wing looked at Luce, despising her. Luce was nothing but a creature from whom to borrow accessories. In this sweet friend, Wing saw no personality, no frailties, no strengths, no goodness, no nothing — just a body.

But then, that was all Wing saw when she looked at Mother.

A maternal body.

Not a real mother, who loved and was loved, who was completely predictable and yet a mystery.

Just a maternal body, a carrier, a wage earner, a car driver.

Dove could not look at the world like that. It was too horrible, too futile and pointless.

Wing left without saying thank you, of course, and Luce tagged along momentarily, hoping for a normal conversation about Timmy, and the date, and where it would lead, and what would happen. But Wing was no longer interested in Luce and did not waste time talking to her. Luce was left standing in her doorway, confused and hurt.

Wing was not using the mouth, and Dove, because it was her friend standing there so pitifully, called back, "Thanks, Luce! See you Monday! I'll tell you all about it then!"

Wing burst out laughing, and their two noises were frightening, a cacophony of unrelated sound.

"Do you know what I'm going to do tomorrow?" said Wing to Dove. "On this little date of yours? With your dull little boyfriend?"

Dove did not know what a viper would find enticing.

"I don't know yet," said Wing, "but it will be

something dramatic. Your life is too boring for me. I want action."

Timmy picked her — or was it them? — up at five A.M.

It was still rather dark, and he had stopped at the convenience store for two coffees to go. He was driving his father's new car, and was full of pride at having been allowed to take it for the morning.

Wing pricked up at this; here was a vulnerable place; the car, perhaps Wing's drama could be through the car, which Timmy, of course, had promised to take perfect care of.

No, please! said Dove on the inside, *let's not hurt the car. Timmy has got to be able to take it back unscratched and unscathed, or his father will kill him.*

So? said Wing.

The lack of interest in her voice was bone-chilling. *You can't kill anybody, Wing,* said Dove.

I was all but dead for fifteen years and nobody cared, said Wing. *Listen,* she added, *you be the one to talk to this jerk. He's too boring for me. I can't be bothered.*

Wing kept the body, but let Dove have the mouth.

How weird it was to be talking to Timmy, and seeing out of the eyes, and yet the hands and body were doing what somebody else felt like doing. Somebody else crossed her knees, fidgeted with the radio, opened the window, and changed the vents.

There were three people in the front seat, but only two of them knew about it.

Timmy, however, was happy. "I love flight," he confided. "I'm going to be a pilot, you know. In fact, for my birthday next summer, my parents are giving me flying lessons. I can hardly wait."

"That's so exciting!" said Dove.

He grinned at her. "I love your voice. The way it changes key. It's like an electronic synthesizer or something."

"It is?"

"Yup. You know. Dial-a-voice. High pitch or low pitch. Sharp edge or Dove edge. Here. Drink your coffee."

But the hand that lay in her lap did not pick up the coffee.

Timmy looked at her.

Wing laughed silently. *I don't feel like coffee, Dove Bar, old twin,* she said. *I'm the one tasting it and swallowing it, and I'm not interested. So there.*

Dove said desperately, "Thanks, Timmy, it was great of you, but I actually am not terribly fond of coffee."

Timmy's face fell. He had been so proud of himself, thinking of it.

Wing's hand picked up the Styrofoam cup, rolled down the window, and threw the whole thing — cup and all — into the grass at the side of the road.

Timmy said tensely, "I hate littering, Dove. Please don't do that again."

Dove hated littering, too. In her head she said, *Wing, I hate you.*

In her head, Wing laughed.

Out loud, Dove said, "I'm sorry, Timmy. I wasn't thinking."

He frowned and drove.

It was going to be a long morning.

They parked in an immense field and hiked through long damp grass to the area where the balloons were tethered. The crews for each balloon were getting ready, and the flames beneath each lovely silk creation were building up hot air, and the balloons were starting to lift. There was much shouting and pulling of ropes and guy wires. The large crowds who had gathered for the display stared in awe as the balloons inflated. How immense they were! How incredibly beautiful!

Like a great box of crayons — every color there ever was. Every pattern, every rainbow.

One went up, then five more, then two, then another half dozen, soaring, lifting, like magnificent Christmas bulbs rejoicing in the sky. The sun rose in the east and its low rays flickered through the dewy grass, sparkled on the black shirt that Dove wore, and turned the balloons into jewels on a velvet sky.

They stared and stared.

"Want to go up in one?" said Timmy, smiling.

Dove shuddered. She didn't like heights.

But Wing was afraid of nothing. "Of course," said Wing.

"Over here," pointed Timmy. "These are the ones that take passengers." They walked to a row of four balloons. A family of three was nervously getting into one basket with a man who would control the balloon. The wife was not sure she really wanted to do this. "Very safe," said the man, smiling. Then, seeing Timmy, he said, "Hey, kid. How are ya? Going up? Who's your friend?"

"This is Dove Daniel," said Timmy proudly, moving her forward like a prize. And to Dove he said, "We don't need to have anybody go with us; I've gone up plenty of times and I know what I'm doing. I'll take you."

Dove opened her mouth to say no, but Wing hurled her out, so that Dove smacked against the back of Wing's mind, hitting the outcroppings of bone, and hurting herself. How is she doing this? thought Dove, dizzy and sick. Do I have to learn how to do this to her as well? Are we going to have wrestling matches of the mind?

Wing said, "I'd love that, Timmy. You're such a sweetie."

Timmy beamed. He launched on a lengthy lecture about aerodynamics, balloon history, how the silk was sewn together. Neither Wing nor Dove listened.

Wing said, *Dove Bar — think of the attention I would get if one of us fell out of the basket!*

Wing! No! You can't do that!

Why not?

Because you'd be dead, that's why! Look how high those balloons are going!

I'm not going to to lose my *balance,* said Wing. Her cruel smile made a terrible blinding light inside their head. Timmy did not see the horrible smile, but the balloon man did, and he flinched.

It's Timmy, said Wing, *who will lose* his *balance.*

Chapter 14

The gondola of the hot air balloon was made of
wicker. It was just a very very large basket. A
sturdy basket, to be sure — but not something
Dove particularly wanted to trust with her life.

In their ancient history book, there was a chapter
on prehistoric England. A scary group of people
lived there when the Romans conquered the island:
Druids. The Romans had crossed the Channel from
France and taken England as a colony two thousand
years ago, and they wrote history books about it.
How strange it was to think of people two thousand
years ago needing to write history books for themselves. How ancient could you get?

Druids, the Romans wrote, made human sacri-
fices. The Druids were not a kindly people and they
did not have kindly gods. They burned people:
women and children and warriors . . . in immense
wicker baskets.

There was an illustration in the history book. One
of those pen-and-ink drawings that can be so much
more horrifying than photographs. It pictured des-

perate victims with their feet on fire. And even as they tried to stomp the fire out, they smothered to death from the smoke.

The Druids had done this often.

There were many periods in history in which nobody would have wanted to live, and this was certainly on the list. Druid sacrifice would have been a very difficult way to die.

Timmy and Wing and Dove entered the basket. Wing's fingers gripped the rough and splintery reeds of the basket, but Dove could not feel it.

There was a fire in this basket. Right in the basket. Flames rose and heat expanded the air to keep the balloon aloft.

Perhaps I was wrong about Wing being from Egypt, thought Dove. Perhaps Wing is really from ancient England. She's a Druid, and she is going to burn us as a sacrifice.

Don't be silly, said Wing inside their shared mind. *If I burn you as a sacrifice, whose body will I have? Nobody's. Don't you understand anything, Dove? I need a body. Yours is the only one I can get at.*

Dove was not fond of heights but, because the body was not hers, she could not feel the lift, or get dizzy from looking down.

She could only look.

Mostly Wing looked straight ahead, so that Dove's view was of the ropes and wires that attached the balloon to the gondola. Sometimes Wing looked at Timmy, and then Dove studied the wide horizontal blue stripes of his shirt. Sometimes Wing stared into the flames, and Dove wanted to squint against the bright orange, but she could not; and Wing did not.

"See?" Timmy kept saying. He kept turning to Wing, laughing with pride, as if he had made the world; this was Timmy's creation, this green and lovely land beneath them. "See the farm?" cried Timmy. And later. "See the village?"

"See the river?" said Wing. "See the playground?"

Wing was mocking him, making Timmy's sentences sound like phrases in a first-grade reader. But Timmy did not know. "Yes!" he cried. "And the road! See the cars?"

"Cars?" said Wing. "Really? On a road? My, my, how exciting, Timmy."

Stop it! said Dove.

Why?

Because you're being ugly, said Dove. *He'll notice, and I don't want him to! I want him to like me.*

Wanting to be liked is one of your personality problems, said Wing. *I don't care about that sort of thing. What I want out of life —* she laughed *— out of your life, Dove — is excitement.*

Wing put her hand in the lower middle of Timmy's back. Timmy turned and smiled at her, dizzy with the excitement of piloting the balloon in front of a girl he adored.

"How high up are we?" asked Wing.

"Not very. A thousand feet."

"That's enough," said Wing.

Enough for what? demanded Dove.

Wing's answering smile was no joyful baby's grin. It was a manic stretching of lips.

"Sure is enough," agreed Timmy. "I like to see details so I don't like to be all that high."

What do you have in mind here? said Dove.

You know what I have in mind, said Wing, *you just don't want to admit it.* Out loud she said. "I think we should throw more ballast out, Timmy, so we can go up higher."

Are you insane? said Dove. *Wing! Answer me! What are you doing?*

I'm not insane. said Wing. *How could I be insane? I'm you.*

Dove fought to get inside the mouth, to use the lungs and tongue and vocal chords to warn Timmy. *She means you, Timmy! You'll be the ballast she throws out!*

Their heart was beating so hard and so fast now, that Dove could feel the thudding all the way up in the skull; every pulse like drums in a marching band. *Don't do it, Wing,* said Dove, *please don't do this.*

I want to, though, said Wing, smiling.

Even if you don't care about killing Timmy, said Dove, *think about what will happen to* you!

Wing was puzzled. *Nothing will happen to me,* she replied.

You'll be a murderer! There will be police and jails and prison and scandal and it will hurt Mother and Father! Think, Wing!

It would not bother me to hurt the maternal body, said Wing. *But surely you know, Dove, that I am*

*not going to any prison or doing any suffering. If
they think it was murder, I'll just go back into your
head and let you take the rap.*

Dove struggled, but she could not invade the
body. Wing had it completely. Dove kicked and
screamed and bit and pounded her fists, but Wing
simply hit the side of her head and otherwise did
not react.

How am I going to warn Timmy? Dove thought.
How can I let him know that he must not turn his
back on me!

On me. Is it me, after all? Are there two of me
in this gondola with Timmy O'Hay?

Timmy, blow me a kiss! Dove tried to cry. It
worked in the classroom. Please, please, blow me
a kiss, set me free, it works in *Sleeping Beauty*!

Wing chatted with Timmy about going up higher.
They had separated from the other balloons. The
sky was empty.

"Let's fly over a city, Timmy," said Wing. "Let's
fly over the mall! I'd love to be right over the mall,
right over that glass pyramid, right where thousands of people are watching us."

She wants to dump him where people are, Dove
realized. It wouldn't attract enough attention if she
dumps him in a hayfield. She wants his body to fall
through the air, and hear the screams of horror from
the people in the parking lots, and hear the smash
when it hits!

Wing, listen to me, she said to her twin, *we can
work this out. Let's strike a bargain. Come on, come
in here and talk to me.*

Timmy said that navigating and steering a hot air balloon was not as simple as driving a car, but he could see something on the horizon and they would head for that.

"Okay," said Wing cheerfully, looking way over the edge.

Dove thought of weird people she had been taught to look through or ignore. People who muttered to themselves, or yanked at their torn and dirty clothing, or slept in doorways. Were they demented? Drunk? Schizophrenic? Drugged?

Or were their bodies in the possession of a vanished twin?

Wing's hands closed around Timmy's waist; he was laughing, pleased that she was showing such enthusiasm.

"Let go of the ropes, Timmy, darling," coaxed Wing, "and give me a kiss."

Timmy let go of the ropes.

No, no, no, please no, thought Dove, please don't let this happen. Let me have a voice, or hands, or something! Anything!

She had no time to wonder why people were afraid of ghosts. What could a ghost do? A ghost had nothing to work with.

The rich farm smell of cows and cut hay reached her nose.

I can smell! thought Dove.

But nobody can be rescued through a sense of smell. To save flesh, you had to have flesh.

Wing pushed.

Chapter 15

A sense of smell.

How strange that so much exists on earth that is not visible. How difficult to identify these things. How much of the world human beings do not possess at all.

Radio waves, curling and wafting in their infinite symmetry . . . waves that bats read, to find their way in the dark . . . waves that whales read, listening to their relatives oceans away.

Colors . . . those ultraviolets human eyes cannot see, but whose presence can burn and fade the skin and the soul.

Sounds . . . those low sonorous murmurs or high unheard whistles that make a dog's ears prick up, while humans sleep on.

A human cannot smell where an animal has marked its territory, but the rest of the living world knows. Deep in the forests, out in the wide mountain meadows, every fox and deer, every woodchuck and chipmunk knows.

Only humans stand ignorant of those invisible inaudible kingdoms.

But this was different. The rich scents that filled Dove's nostrils belonged to her; she knew them; she had names for them: cut hay, turned earth, burning gas, fragrant flowers, boys' sweat.

Dove was back in Dove.

She clung to Timmy's shirt. Oh, the joy of feeling the cotton against her fingers! The inexpressible joy of looking where she chose to look! Saying what she wanted to say. Moving where she wanted to move!

A smell saved us, thought Dove. A smell brought me back. Some perfume of the earth was strong enough to oppose some perfume of evil.

"I'm sorry," she said, "I lost my balance. I'm scared, Timmy. Let's land. Please?"

Timmy maneuvered the ropes. "Okay," he said in a funny collapsed voice. "The field on the other side of that brook would be perfect."

But what smell? thought Dove. Of all the million smells in the world, ones I can identify and ones I can't, which smell brought me back? Cut hay, turned earth, burning gas, fragrant flowers, boys' sweat? All or a combination? Or one I didn't even know I was sniffing?

There is an antidote. I know that now, but I can't be going up in hot air balloons to sniff for it every time Wing gets back in control.

First, Timmy was saying, he had to look and see if there was anything important growing in the field, because they weren't supposed to land where farmers' crops would be ruined; no, he could see a horse at the far end of the field, near a white fence; so it was pasture; except that he might scare the horse, and that would be terrible; he could never face the farmor, lot alone ask to use his phono, if the horse went beserk with fear and broke loose, or broke his leg trying.

The burst of speech from Timmy was so incredibly beautiful.

And Dove, too, had speech! A mouth, lips, tongue, vocal chords, throat. Thank you! thought Dove. Thank you for all the body has and does and is!

Dove looked down at herself, at the miracle that is the human body. She curled her fingers with ecstasy: The fingers belonged to her, she could control them, they would obey! Dove could not help laughing a little, joy pouring out of her. The body was awesome! To be alive again, to have flesh as well as soul — it was the most beautiful thing on earth.

I'm okay, she thought, I'm back. I don't know exactly what happened, but I'm here again. Oh, thank you, thank you, thank you!

Don't think you've won, said Wing, fierce and sharp and full of hate.

Dove was cocky. She had come back in time. *And why not?* she said snippily to Wing. *I have.*

You've won this time. But not the next.

You won't be coming back, said Dove. *I'm too strong. Too here.*

Yes, I will come back. Hesta still has the VENOM.

I'm not friends with Hesta, Dove pointed out.

You're in class with Hesta, though.

And you're not! So there!

Timmy said, "Dove? Are you okay?"

Dove froze. Had she been talking out loud? Had Wing been using her mouth at the same time? Had Timmy listened to their conversation?

Nobody would understand that there were two living in the head. Nobody would be sympathetic.

She stole a glance at Timmy. He looked freaked.

Which of us is the freak? thought Dove. Am I so far gone that I can't even tell if I'm talking out loud? Have I become one of those weird people sleeping on streets, muttering to myself, and jerking at my hair and my clothes? "I'm fine, Timmy. Just glad we're down."

"We're not down, Dove," said Timmy quietly.

Dove had been so busy smelling and breathing, she had forgotten to look at anything. There was as much sky around her as before. She was as wrapped in blue as if she had been swimming in the Mediterranean.

Or the Nile.

Timmy was not looking at her with affection. He was looking at her with anxiety.

No . . .

. . . *with fear.*

Inside the head, Wing laughed and laughed. *Timmy half knew*, she said. *He half realized I was going to push him. He can't quite believe it. But he can't quite unbelieve it, either. Look at his eyes,*

Dovey. See how wrecked they are. He's scared, Dovey. Of us.

Wing reveled in it. She had scared somebody within an inch of his life and it had made her happy.

Only pushing Timmy out would have made her happier.

When they finally landed, and the family in whose yard they landed came running out, thrilled to see their first hot air balloon, telling Timmy of course he could use their phone to call the truck to come get them. . . . Dove knew that Wing had ended the tiny romance.

Timmy was afraid of her.

Timmy — whose hand she wanted to hold, whose lips she wanted to kiss — Timmy kept carefully to the far side of the room, and the far side of the truck cab that carried them back to the fairgrounds, and when they were going home, kept also to the far side of his car.

Neither person said a word the whole drive back to Sky Change Hills Condominiums. Radios are so useful. The noise, the patter of the deejay, the melody and the percussion and the synthesized chords. These took the place of romance and conversation. The radio played on and on.

Timmy dropped her off in front of the complex.

"Wouldn't you like to come in?" said Dove. She tacked a nervous smile on her face. "I mean, we left so early for the liftoff that it's not even noon yet. Let's have a sandwich."

Timmy tacked a nervous smile on his face, too.

"No, thanks," he said. Politely. Much too politely. "Got to go home and mow the lawn."

"Oh, I forgot lawns," said Dove. "Living in a condo complex, you forget stuff like that."

"Yeah, you do," said Timmy. He kept both hands on the wheel. He was waiting for her to get out and shut the door so he could drive away.

Please don't let this be over! thought Dove. Let me think of something interesting to say, something that will make him laugh, and like me again! She swallowed. Some of the thoughts in her head belonged to Wing. Oh, the unfairness of it! She did not even dare to speak, lest Wing's words emerge, lest Wing's terrible personality come out of Dove's throat like tainted water.

Timmy sat very still.

She put her hand on the door handle and pulled the small metal lever toward herself, and the door opened and the automatic seat belt slid neatly away from her chest. Timmy said, "Well, thanks for coming. Have a nice weekend. See you around."

She got a grip on her thoughts and her mouth. With great care she kept Wing from speaking for her. "Thank you for asking me," Dove said. "It was very exciting." Please, Timmy, look at me? See Dove in this body and not Wing? Please?

But he did not look up and he did not see Dove. He drove away with controlled care, as if revving the motor or shifting gears too fast would form a net around him, condemning him to the personality he had felt in the wicker basket.

Dove stood on the sidewalk outside the complex.

She was exhausted.

Her cramped, crowded, aching head felt alone. She did not have the slightest sense of Wing. Am I alone in here after all? thought Dove. I don't feel occupied. I don't think she's in there.

Dove was so tired she felt as if Wing must have taken all the energy when she left. She dissolved again, thought Dove, she's vanished a second time. I wonder where she went.

Timmy's car turned the corner. He was out of sight now. There was hard-packed earth between him and the girl who might — he half believed — have tried to toss him out a thousand feet above the ground. Timmy shifted almost violently into third, tires crying out against the hot pavement, then wrenched the gears into fourth, gravel flicking up from under his tires. Dove could hear the pebbles dancing, long after Timmy's car was gone.

She dragged herself into the complex.

The rows of apartments seemed terribly far away and small. They might have been built of Legos. She might have been a plastic doll with plastic legs with only a fraction of the necessary joints.

She trudged into her own house. It was cool and quiet. The soft gray colors and carpets made it seem more like a hospital or a rest home. Her parents' various means of communication were flickering: red lights on the answering machine, paper gently drifting out of the fax machine. A note from each parent lay on the stairs so that she would be sure to see the messages on the way up to her room.

Hope you didn't fall out of the balloon or any-

thing! said her father's note. *I went golfing with a client. Home around dinner. Love you.*

Hope you had a wonderful time, darling, said her mother's note. *I went in to work today, will be home around dinner. A friend of yours dropped off a package for you. It's on the kitchen table. Love you.*

Dove perked up a little. She loved the word *package*. It sounded secret and special: brown paper hiding a treat. Perhaps she would go into the kitchen, make herself something yummy to eat, and open the package.

She was disappointed to see that it was not a real package, with tape and twine and extra postage, but a brown paper lunch bag, twisted at the top. It had fallen on its side and whatever was in it had spilled.

Venom.

Chapter 16

If only Hesta had not brought the bottle of *Venom* to the house!

If only it had not tipped over and spilled.

If only . . .

But you could go on forever with your *if only*'s and none of them would change the fact that Wing was back, with a leaden permanence that Dove could not combat.

Wing was rude to Mother and Father. She played upon their weaknesses and their worries, and easily punctured their pride and joy. For fifteen years Mother and Father and Dove had led a quiet existence, speaking little, hugging less, and yet fond of each other, in their separate ways.

Wing laughed at Father, trying to learn languages in the car. "You work for a stupid telephone company," she said, "in the billing department. You will never earn enough money to travel. So what is with this pretense that you're learning Japanese and German? You know ten words in each language."

Wing punctured Mother, whose magazines invariably featured articles like "Does Mother Damage Her Children by Working?" "If you weren't so focused on your pathetic little fax machine," said Wing, "and your grubby little clients, you'd know a little more about me. If anything goes wrong with me, you know, it's your fault."

Wing began addressing Mother and Father as Maternal Body and Paternal Body. She would laugh and taunt them when she did it, and Mother and Father would cringe and flinch. They did not yell back, or scold, or punish. They did not really know how. It had never been necessary before.

Wing's eyes, backlit with hatred, scared them.

"Dove," Mother would say helplessly, "why are you so angry at us?"

"Dove," Father would say anxiously, "what happened to our sweet dear daughter? Where does this hostility come from?"

How ambivalent these word wars made Dove. Her parents missed her. The twin they had wanted to have was home, and they didn't like it. That felt good. But her parents were hurt, crushed, frightened. That felt bad. It was as nauseating to swing between good and bad, as to swing from earth to sky, upside down in a roller coaster.

As Dove grew smaller, her fighting spirit lessened, until it was just a spark, impossible to light from within. She made occasional token protests, but mostly Dove let Wing go her way.

"It would be pleasant to destroy any of your friends," said Wing. "It's a matter of deciding which one. Connie, of course, is vain and self-centered, and probably easier to damage than Luce, who is energetic and will be harder to pierce. But Luce would be more of a challenge. It's more fun to destroy a virtuous person than a bad one. After all, a bad one is going to self-destruct one day anyhow. So probably I will ruin Luce."

"Please, Wing. They haven't done anything to you."

"What does that have to do with it? They are victims waiting to be taken."

Victim. What a dreadful word. Somebody selected to be damaged. "Wing, tell me why anybody should be a victim?"

"I want revenge."

"For what?" cried Dove. "If you have to take over my body and my life, why can't you just enjoy it?"

Wing did not seem to know the meaning of the word *enjoy*.

They arrived at the school.

Mr. Phinney was just going in the west entrance. He waved and yelled but was too far away to hear Wing's terrible answer. That's the revenge, thought Dove, understanding a little bit. Mr. Phinney *was* just absent; for him the perfume was no different from the stink of locker rooms; it didn't touch him at all. He had no vanished twin waiting to emerge.

Venom didn't get him. Wing didn't get him.

Which meant that Wing would want to get someone else.

Connie and Luce waved and headed Dove's way.

Of course it was not Dove, it was Wing; and Wing had no use for conventions like saying hello or answering questions. Wing simply moved on into the building discussing which victim to take.

"Timmy was fun," said Wing. "I loved scaring him to death. I think that was more fun than actually doing him to death, you know."

Dove didn't believe that for a minute. Wing would have pushed Timmy out if Dove had not managed to return. At first, Dove had dreamed endlessly of returning again. Now she hardly ever thought of return. It seemed so unlikely that the antidote to *Venom* would drift her way again, or that she would be awake enough, or determined enough, to snatch it.

To be without a body, the ultimate prison, was a form of death.

"I think," mused Wing, "that I will return to Timmy. Danger is intoxicating and although Timmy is nervous now, he is also drawn. The unbelieving half of him is in the ascendant."

"What horoscope are you talking about?" said Connie, puzzled.

Wing continued to address Dove. "Timmy has overcome the handicap of being ugly and turned it to an advantage. Male movie stars often do that; I can think of several TV series in which the star is ugly, and yet he manages to be sexy and attractive, too." Wing smiled. "Yes, I believe I will ruin Timmy. That would be satisfying."

"Dove, what are you babbling about?" said Luce. "You sound awful."

Dove was merely resident in the brain, like a parasite. She could not talk to Luce, nor explain, nor change voices. She did not even feel particularly emotional; Wing, whose emotions, like hate, were as strong as crimson and blood, had swamped Dove's sweet, soft, pastel emotions.

Connie kept trying to get Dove to talk to her. Through Wing's eyes, Dove watched Connie's mouth flap. Wing was not interested in Connie and remained silent. It was Hesta with whom Wing talked.

Connie was hurt. She looked from Dove to Luce, hoping for an explanation but none came.

"Let's go shopping after school, Hesta," said Wing.

Although she had always despised Dove, Hesta took this in stride. Hesta accepted the new personality completely and eagerly. Connie did not. Eyes full of pain, Connie stared beseechingly at the girl she thought was her friend. I'm sorry, thought Dove helplessly, but it isn't me. It's Wing.

Luce said, "Dove — aren't you sitting with us at lunch?"

Wing laughed.

"I've come to my senses, dumbo," said Wing.

Luce and Connie were out of Dove's vision but she heard their voices: "Is Dove on something?" whispered Connie, weeping at the back of her voice.

Luce said, "She's just being rotten. Forget her."

Forget her.

A sort of terror spread through Dove — whatever relic of Dove remained now. Her two best friends would forget her. How easy it would be for them, because Wing was not going to leave a single trace of Dove.

Wing dismissed Connie and Luce as if she were brushing ants off her food at a picnic, and went with Hesta. Hesta disdained cafeteria food; it was too disgusting for her to consume. But Hesta would never bring lunch with her, either, because that was too common. Hesta got a candy bar, a soda, and a bright red apple out of the vending machines and linked arms with Wing and they went outside together to talk about pitiful rejects like Connie and Luce.

"Oh, give me a break!" Wing said. "Can you believe I used to hang out with them? Please!" Wing and Hesta laughed hysterically, looking back at Connie and Luce, and laughing even more.

Don't say things like that out loud, thought Dove. I have to come back here, you know. What will I do for friends when it's my turn again?

It won't be your turn again, you fool, said Wing. I am here, and I am here to stay, and I am going to make good use of your body.

It won't be my turn again? thought Dove. She stared out the narrow opening of Wing's eyes. There was nothing to see but Hesta, and Hesta's mean superior crowd, and Hesta's big grabby hands.

I don't want to look at this, thought Dove. She tried to close her eyes, but that was not within her control, and she was stuck there, watching, unblinking unless Wing chose to blink.

"Among other things on my agenda," said Wing to Hesta, "such as skipping Luce and Connie, and destroying Timmy, and acquiring a new wardrobe, is getting a new name."

Hesta cocked her head, very birdlike. But not dovelike. She was a crow, perhaps, pecking at a roadkill. "Dove is a pathetic excuse for a name," agreed Hesta.

No, thought Dove, don't rename me! Nothing will be left of me.

"I'll think up a perfect name," said Wing, "and we'll inform everybody what they're going to call me in the future."

Hesta and Wing went to the mall in Hesta's car. Hesta had a wonderful car; at any other time Dove would have been awestruck. Now she just wished Hesta would have an accident. Hit a slick place on the road. Take Wing with her.

But if there was an accident . . . and this body I used to own got killed . . . what would happen to me? What is a soul? How much does the body really matter? Are Wing and I two? Or have we completely merged? Are we one? Were we always one?

I didn't ask for this and I don't think it's fair, God, thought Dove.

Wing said irritably, "It's extremely fair. Think how you locked me up for fifteen years, Dove."

"I love the way you do that," said Hesta.

"Do what?" said Wing.

"Talk to yourself like that. As if Dove were somebody else."

"She is," said Wing. "Here, let's go in this store."

Ragged Rock. *The* store for strange clothing: clothing with rips or fringes, shimmering mirrors or rusted metal strips, Indian beads, clashing colors or amazing neon brilliance.

Nothing would have made Dove touch any fabric in Ragged Rock. She sank into the bottom of the mind. She didn't want to see these clothes draped over her body.

"Look down there," said Hesta suddenly, pointing over the mall atrium and down into the lower level. "There's your mom."

"No," said Wing.

"What do you mean — no?" Hesta pointed again. "Next to the Kitchen Shoppe. See? It's your mother."

"No. It's the maternal body. It's Dove's mother."

Hesta giggled. "I love it when you talk like that. 'The maternal body.' As if all it did was give birth. That's how I feel about my mother."

It's not how I feel about mine! thought Dove. I love my mother.

Hesta and Wing leaned on the glass balustrade and looked down into the atrium.

Dove's mother switched packages from one hand to the other and walked, without ever looking up, into the department store and disappeared behind the perfume counter.

Perfume.

Memories of perfumes once sniffed were as strong as memories of Christmas mornings once unwrapped.

Mother! thought Dove, wanting to go home, and be little, and be safe.

Wing trembled. Dove felt it long before Hesta saw it: a queer shudder in every cell of the body, a rippling of thought and molecule. Wing tipped back, staring up into the glass pyramid. The yellow sun shone down into her eyes with such ferocity that Dove felt herself turning gold.

Wing's trembling took possession of her entire body, and she convulsed, rippling, each muscle in turn shuddering.

Wing held her hands up to the blue sky outside the glass pyramid, and seemed to wait for some answer. Then slowly Wing walked away, elegantly, like a one-person procession. She stood on the top step of the escalator and was borne down like a queen on a palanquin.

Hesta said nervously, "Dove?"

"I'm not Dove," said Wing softly. She pressed her palms together, and held them upward, as if offering a sacrifice. Her body continued to ripple and quake, like a robot whose bolts were coming apart.

Through the glitter of the sun in her eyes, Dove saw fear on the shoppers' faces. Who was this girl dressed in black, body quivering like a volcano ready to explode, hands held up as if she were a sniper reaching for a machine gun?

Wing never blinked.

Never looked down.

When she reached the bottom, she walked directly into the splashing fountain. She did not see the shoppers who paused, and stared, and exchanged frightened glances. She held her hands up to the pyramid's cone straight above her and called the gods of the Nile. "I know you're there!" cried Wing. "I can see you!"

She dipped her hands into the cool tumbling water and threw droplets of silver into the air toward the pyramid.

Yes! thought Dove. Go! Take your ancient twisted genes and go back to the Nile, back to Egypt, back to your tomb! Just leave me here! Dove tried to fall back in the mind to give Wing room to fly, to let Wing out of whatever opening Wing had come in.

Like falling autumn leaves, Dove heard whispery flutters of talk among the people staring at this strange event. Dove saw Wing as the crowd leaning over the second-floor railings saw her: a small slim girl, shrieking nonsense about wings. A girl floating on the edge of insanity, baptizing herself in a mall fountain.

"What's going on?"

"Who is that girl?"

"Somebody call the mall police!"

Don't call them yet, thought Dove. Give Wing a minute. This might work, she might go. Please let her go!

"Don't get involved!" said a harsh voice. "Wait for the ambulance. They know how to handle this stuff. Sometimes people like that get violent."

Another *v* word. There was no end to these *v*

words. Dove floated in *v* words: venom, viper, victim, violence.

"What will happen to her?" said a shopper. "It's not a crime, is it?"

"Lock her up, I suppose. Their personalities snap like that, they don't get 'em back, you know."

The shoppers knew. They had an extra show that day; how they enjoyed it. They circled her.

I'm glad I'm safe inside, thought Dove, cringing. Those are scary people out there.

Hesta's big long hands closed on Wing's shoulders. "Are you crazy?" hissed Hesta. "It was funny at first, but enough's enough."

Wing ignored her.

"Let's get out of here!" said Hesta.

Wing continued to shriek, but now the words were not English, they were something far more primitive, something ancient and evil.

"Stand away from her!" shouted somebody. "She's flipped out."

"Come on," hissed Hesta. Grabbing Wing's shoulder did not work, so she grabbed Wing's hair. "Come on!"

"You touched me," said Wing.

"We have to get out of here!" said Hesta, yanking at her.

"You touched me," said Wing. "You'll be sorry."

Chapter 17

Safely in Hesta's car, dripping on the lovely wine-red upholstery, Wing continued to tremble under the spell of whatever she had seen through the sun and the glass.

Hesta, too, was trembling, driving quickly, looking over her shoulder, muttering, "Dove, who would have thought you could get so weird?"

Dove seemed to be the body also; she felt damp on the seat and the curliness of her hair from being under the fountain. She felt the pressure of the shoulder strap and the acceleration of the curve.

She knew what was happening. Wing was receding just enough for Dove to take the blame. Wing would let Dove suffer for what Wing had done.

It is hard enough to take the consequences for what you do yourself — but to take the consequences for what your other personality does? How unfair!

People will assume that it was *me* in that fountain. *I'll* have to pay the price. It'll be my mother and father who have to deal with it. Not some maternal body. My mother! And what will Wing do?

Wing will vanish.

"You looked so funny in that fountain," said Hesta. "There you were, splashing like a two-year-old, calling up to the sky like you're worshipping the mall gods, or something! What a hoot! Too bad nobody had a video, because everybody at school would love it. You used to be so stodgy, Dove! And now you're halfway to an insane asylum."

Hesta was teasing. Dove recognized the lilt.

But it was Wing to whom she was really talking, and Wing did not like being teased. Wing's inner trembling was replaced by a metallic brittleness, as if neither Wing nor Dove owned the body anymore — it was a robot's. The bolts were being tightened. Wing's eyes drilled into Hesta's.

Dove shrank back from the force of Wing's dislike.

"You have such a creepy expression on your face," giggled Hesta.

"Are you afraid?" said Wing. "You should be."

Hesta laughed so hard, she hardly kept hold of the steering wheel, but controlled it with the tips of two fingers. "You looked so funny at the mall," giggled Hesta. "At the time I admit it shook me a little, but now that we've got away, and nobody could possibly have recognized you, Dove Bar, I mean your own mother wouldn't have recognized you — well, the truth is, you looked so funny."

The venom that was Wing turned her pale with hatred for Hesta.

Hesta paused at a red light and took in Wing's

expression. "What are you thinking about?" she said, giggling again.

"I am," said Wing, "choosing my next victim."

Hesta giggled on, hearing nothing wrong in that sentence. "Oh, Dove, you're so funny! I mean, I had no idea. You hung out with Luce, who's so annoying, and Connie, who's so simple-minded. And here you are, you're so funny, Dove Bar."

"I am not Dove," said Wing through her teeth. "I am Wing."

"Wing, schming," said Hesta. "Say, there's Timmy O'Hay and Laurence. Let's pass them." Hesta slammed down the accelerator. She pulled into the left lane and drew up next to Timmy. Timmy looked over, saw Dove in the passenger seat, saw Hesta driving, and took the challenge. He floored the gas. Hesta and Timmy roared down the road, neck and neck, stock car racing in the middle of town.

"What do you mean — Wing schming?" said Wing.

"Stupid name," said Hesta.

Call me stupid! Wing said silently. *I'll show you stupid, Hesta!*

"Stick with Dove," advised Hesta. "You're giving 'Dove' a whole new meaning."

I'm going to give you a whole new meaning, said Wing silently.

Don't do anything, Dove pleaded. *We're going too fast.*

"Go faster, Hesta," said Wing. "Timmy's going

to beat us." Because they shared a mind, Dove knew what Wing was thinking of. Because Dove looked out the same eyes, Dove knew what Wing was looking at.

The steering wheel.

A strange sense of lassitude overcame Dove, as if she had been given sleeping medicine. Wing was not only going to do something stupid, she was going to do something dangerous. Something potentially fatal. Something vicious, with victims.

One of the victims would certainly be Hesta.

One of the victims could be Timmy O'Hay. One Laurence.

And one, though Wing seemed not to understand the consequences, could be Dove.

Dove could curl up and take a nap inside the mind. What was the point in worrying? She had no more control than an infant in a car seat has control of what happens to the car.

Dove could not even look over and check out Timmy, see if he was still racing Hesta, because Wing's eyes were focused on the steering wheel that Hesta held loosely in her hands.

Wing cast a quick glance over the traffic patterns of the road ahead and made her decision. She was going to wrench the wheel when they drove over a raised portion of the road, where daisies bloomed like a million white and yellow stars, and the road edge fell twenty feet to a rock-lined gully.

Your thoughts are too horrible. I don't want to

share thoughts any more, Dove said.

Then don't listen, said Wing. Evil filled the cavity of their mind.

I wasn't brought up like this, thought Dove. I was brought up to be kind and do right. How did Wing turn out bad? She was there with me all along. Why didn't she learn the same things from Mother and Father that I learned?

Or was she there all along? Is she really my vanished twin? Do such things happen?

Or is she some evil spirit from the ancient past, who came through the skylight, or through the *Venom* or through whatever terrible powers are out there? Invisible and uncaring?

They were parallel to Timmy's car. If Wing went ahead with her plan, they'd crash into Timmy and both cars would careen over the edge, smashing the wildflowers and smashing each other.

Or is there no Wing at all? thought Dove Daniel, dwindled and diminished in the back of the mind.

Just me . . . going insane.

Chapter 18

"Don't do it, Wing," Dove said.

"Go back to sleep," said Wing.

"I'm your victim," said Dove. "I accept that. But nobody else should be your victim, Wing."

"I'm in control. What I choose is what will happen," said Wing. She flexed her hand, preparing.

But Hesta had grabbed the wheel herself, tightening her hands till her knuckles were white, wrenching the wheel a different direction, skidding into the parking lot of a doughnut shop. The brakes slammed, the key turned, and Hesta popped out of the car. Out of breath, staring at Dove with the same look of fear that Timmy had worn, Hesta said brightly, "Well! Let's have a snack. Jelly doughnut? Coke? Coffee?"

Hesta had heard both conversations. Both Wing and Dove had spoken aloud, arguing both sides of whether to give Hesta a fatal accident.

Wing's hope for excitement and horror vanished. She sat sullenly under the seat belt.

"Cruller," added Hesta. "Powdered sugar. Glazed."

Perfect word, thought Dove. You do look a little glazed.

"What are you, a waitress?" said Wing. "I don't like doughnuts."

"Fine," said Hesta. "Well, of course, now that we're here, I guess I'm just going to go in and have one anyway." Hesta looked as if she might spend several hours in there, safe among the doughnuts, rather than do any more driving with Wing.

One way to end an unfortunate friendship, thought Dove.

"I wanted to end it a different way," said Wing.

Hesta fled.

Dove said aloud, "You realize that when we talk to each other, everybody can hear."

"I like it that way," replied Wing. "I like to watch their faces when they realize there are two of us in one body. I like how they flinch."

"Even though Hesta laughed at you," said Dove, "I think you should feel gratitude to her and not hurt her."

"Gratitude?" said Wing. "In the mall, you mean? Please, Dove. She interrupted something very important there."

Dove waited, but Wing did not say what important thing had been going on, other than a humiliating display. "Gratitude because she was the one who opened *Venom* again," said Dove. "I'm not grateful, of course, but you should be."

"Gratitude is such a human kind of thing, don't you think?" said Wing.

"Aren't you human?" said Dove. She was slipping into a coma of despair. Wing was going to kill somebody, and it would look like Dove had done it!

"No."

"Dove, we are so worried about you," said Luce.

"I'm not worried about you," said Wing. "You're easy prey. When I decide to take you, I'll take you."

Wing discussed her failure to push Timmy out of the gondola.

She discussed her failure to turn Hesta's steering wheel.

She discussed her conversation with Egypt at the bottom of the pyramid in the mall.

Nobody else had much else to say. Especially Timmy and Hesta.

It was not surprising that Mr. Phinney, the ancient history teacher, suggested Dove might want to go to the nurse, as she seemed to be fatigued. Being Mr. Phinney, he actually said, "You seem very very very fatigued to me, Dove."

Wing raised her eyebrows high enough to take flight on them.

Mr. Phinney said, "I think you have been working very very very hard, Dove, and you just need rest. Sometimes we get overextended, we just take on far far far too much, and we need to be couch potatoes for a while, rest our bodies and our minds."

"Dove is resting," explained Wing. "I'm here instead. I expect I'll be here for some time. It's the perfume, you know."

"An aspirin and a half hour's rest," recommended Mr. Phinney, and both Dove and Wing laughed at that. Their two laughs spiralled insanely in the thick classroom air.

The school psychologist happened to be in that afternoon; this seemed unfair to Dove, since he came only one afternoon a week.

"Now, Dove," said the school psychologist. "Tell me what's wrong."

"I've been planning how to destroy Timmy," said Wing. "Thinking up the most effective technique."

"Why," said the psychologist, "would you want to destroy Timmy?"

"Why not?" said Wing. She smiled, and the psychologist flinched, just the way Wing liked it. With all his experience he had not dealt with a teenager like this.

He was afraid of her.

How am I going to escape this mess? thought Dove. I can't even get out of my body.

The psychologist made phone calls. Wing seemed not to know the purpose of them, but Dove found them very clear: He was going to lock Dove up. She was mentally ill, and he was going to take away her freedom.

I'm not mentally ill, you have to understand that, it's the perfume. It summoned Wing from inside of me and she's in charge now! It's a vanished twin. It's evil. It isn't me. Don't take it out on me.

"Sometimes," said the school psychologist, "a

half hour of rest isn't quite enough, you know, my dear. Sometimes we need several weeks. Even several months. Lots and lots of rest."

I've already lost my freedom! thought Dove. I don't even have a body. Please, please, please, no, don't put me in an institution!

"An institution," said the school pychologist, "can be a great help in times of trouble such as these."

Terror seized Dove like the talons of a hawk, deep and sharp.

Wing, amused, proceeded to frighten the psychologist more.

Dove's mother and father were summoned from work to discuss their daughter.

"The maternal body," said Wing, raising her eyebrows to ceiling heights. "My goodness — it left work for my sake. What sacrifice."

"The maternal body?" repeated the psychologist carefully.

"Hello, Dove, honey," said her parents, terrified and worried.

"I am Wing," said Wing, introducing herself.

On the inside, Dove was as weak as a single piece of confetti; a tiny circle of colored paper. She felt as if even gravity would have nothing to do with her; she was too light for the world.

Mother! she thought. Father! Get me out of here! You gave birth to me before — you have to give birth to me again.

"What did she say?" whispered her mother. *"Wing?"*

"There is no Wing, sweetheart," said her father carefully. "That was just a story."

"You should be so lucky," said Wing.

The room was very quiet.

"I was unfit, you know," said Wing. "The maternal body often discards an unborn that is unfit."

Mother and Father were practically comatose with horror. Dove knew how they felt.

I have to summon up my strength, thought Dove. Pull myself together and get rid of Wing. When we go home tonight, somehow I'll break the bottle of *Venom* into the sink, and wash it away, and that will be the end of Wing.

"You will do no such thing," said Wing. "I am the perfume and the perfume is me, and I am here to stay. I am Wing."

"Oh, my god," whispered Dove's mother. "She's having some sort of nervous breakdown."

"No, I'm not," said Wing. "I'm simply here at last. You missed me and now I'm here. You should be glad to see me. What's the matter with you, anyway?"

Dove's mother clutched Dove's father's hand. There were two of them, and it gave them strength. There are two of us, too, thought Dove, but it doesn't give me strength.

"I never did like the maternal body," Wing told the psychologist. He flinched again. Wing smiled again.

"I'm going to recommend a mild tranquillizer," said the psychologist, "and she should stay home tomorrow and rest. Let's hope this is simply a brief episode."

"There is nothing simple about it," said Wing. "*You* are simple. Your *solutions* are simple. For that matter, the maternal and paternal bodies are simple. But I myself — No. I am not simple."

Simple, thought Dove on the inside. Simple, mimple, pimple, himple. This time the words poked out. "Simple, mimple, pimple, himple," said the mouth rhythmically and repetitively. Both Wing and Dove were surprised at the jumble of words pouring past the tongue.

"On the other hand," said the psychologist, "I could call the acute ward at the city hospital and see if they would evaluate her."

"No, no, no," said Dove's mother quickly. "We'll just drive on home and I'm sure we'll settle down." Her mother looked at her watch. "Tomorrow at work will be very very very important," she said fretfully. "I can't believe the timing on this."

"Very, very, very," said the mouth. "I never believe anybody who uses three very's in a row. Very, very, very. Very, very, very. Very, very, very."

Is that me talking? thought Dove. Or Wing?

The school psychologist said perhaps Dove's timing was purposeful; had Dove known tomorrow was a very important day? Was Dove perhaps resentful of her parents' work? Was this her method of —

"No," said Wing. "I have absolutely no interest in their work, or in them, for that matter. I split fifteen years ago."

The psychologist whistled under his breath, as though to give himself support. "I definitely feel the hospital . . . "

But her parents had Dove by the arms and were hustling her out of the building. Dove could not feel the pressure on the arms but through Wing's eyes she could see the speed at which they were leaving the school building.

Immediately, there was a logistical problem. Each parent had driven. Which car to use? Neither parent wanted the burden of the daughter alone.

The blossoming shrubs of late spring formed a bright hedge near the parking lot. Her parents brushed past the leaves and drooping flowers. A sweet old-fashioned smell, like an old lady's dresser drawer lined with paper, filled the air. Wing held a hand over her face trying not to breathe.

Dove came to her senses.

No — they came to her. The senses were smells. The antidote! Whatever it was — this was it.

Dove kicked and screamed and pounded on the prison of the brain. The heart doubled its beating, and Dove kicked harder, demanding oxygen, demanding air. Wing yanked open the nearest car door, trying to get into the artificial air, but she did not make it.

Sweet romantic fragrance filled Dove's nostrils, then her head, then dreamily swept her into the real world. "Antidote," breathed Dove.

"Only seasonally," said Wing.

Two separate voices were coming out of Dove

now: her own and Wing's. Dove didn't mind; she knew Wing was receding.

Her parents minded.

In the car going home, Dove kept saying, "Don't worry, Mother. It's under control."

In *her* voice, Wing kept saying, "I will get control back. Don't think that you have won."

"Shut up!" shouted Dove. And then, gently, "Don't worry, Mother. Wing will stop talking in a bit. At first you're both in the mouth, but then you fall backward. It's a little scary because it's such a long way down, but it doesn't hurt. You just lie there in the back of the brain and wait your turn." She smiled at her mother.

Her mother smiled back.

It was identical to the smiles of Timmy and Hesta.

It was not a smile.

It was a tremor of fear.

Chapter 19

"I do not have a multiple personality!" cried Dove. "I am just me! Nobody else."

"Then who is holding the other side of the conversation?" said the psychiatrist in a soothing, humor-the-maniac voice. Her parents had not retained the school psychologist. Everybody knew that the school psychologists were both incompetent and gossipy. The Daniels needed an expert who would tell nobody anything about their daughter.

"My vanished twin," said Dove. "Wing."

"Wing," repeated the psychiatrist. "That's a strange name."

"It her real name."

"Her real name," repeated the psychiatrist.

"My parents named her!" cried Dove. "Before I was born. Ask them. It is true. I am not making anything up."

"Before you were born," repeated the psychiatrist.

"My mother was due to have twins," said Dove,

trying to remain calm. The doctor's examining room, ominously, was within the gates of a place called Cherry Valley Hospital: We treat the chemically dependent, the abused, and the confused. I'm not chemically dependent, thought Dove, the only person who's ever abused me is Wing, and I'm not confused, the doctor is. "About halfway through her pregnancy," explained Dove with desperate necessary care, "they found she was going to have only one baby after all. It's called the vanishing twin syndrome. I'm sure you've heard of it."

The psychiatrist nodded for some time. Slowly he said, "Did you see this on a daytime television talk show, perhaps? Did it excite you?"

Dove closed her eyes. "It is not exciting," she said. "It is scary, don't you understand? *There is somebody else living in my head.*"

"In your head," he repeated.

Closing her eyes had been an error. Her grip on the world was momentarily weakened. Wing leaped back into the mouth. "What did you learn in medical school?" demanded Wing. "How to imitate other people?"

He smiled. "It's a good technique, Dove. You've told me quite a lot, haven't you?"

"I've told you a lot, but you haven't understood a lot. Like for example, I am not Dove. I am Wing. You should be able to tell the difference. I find it insulting that you still confuse us. Dove is the goody-goody."

The psychiatrist steepled his fingers and studied

the way the pads of one hand rested against the pads of the other hand. "And what does that make you, Wing?" he said.

Don't tell him about trying to push Timmy out of the hot air balloon, said Dove silently. *You don't want him to lock us up, do you?*

What do you mean, lock us up? said Wing.

Where do you think we are, you nincompoop? said Dove. *We are in the examining room of a private psychiatric hospital. Mother and Father are in the waiting area. All they have to do is sign a paper and we are stuck here, you and I. We will have to live here!*

So? said Wing.

So, I don't want to live in a mental institution. Not even for a night. Let alone a lifetime. I want to go to school and be normal.

Wing shook her head. Their head. Whichever head it was. Dove had lost track of who possessed the body. They seemed to be merging. Wing said, *I don't think you'll ever be normal again, Dove. Not when I can come back at will.*

The psychiatrist said, "I think I'm going to ask Mom and Dad to come in with us for a minute."

"I don't call them Mom and Dad," said Dove.

"I know. You call them the maternal body and the paternal body."

"I do not! I call them Mother and Father!"

The psychiatrist nodded. He brought Dove's parents into the room. He said, "I'd like to play you a tape of your daughter's conversation with me."

"You taped me?" yelled Wing. "I haven't just

been sitting here for the last fifteen years, you know, waiting for *Venom* to come! I've been paying attention! You cannot tape a person's conversation without that person's permission! You cheated."

"*Venom*," said the psychiatrist, "seems to be your daughter's excuse for having developed a double personality. It's a very frightening word for a little girl to choose. She seems to realize that in some way, because she identifies it as a perfume, even though it's a snake poison."

Dove's parents held each other's hands, but not Dove's.

"You have a very sick girl," said the psychiatrist. He played a tape for them. The Daniel family listened to the double voices, like a flute and a cello duet, Wing up high and Dove down low, arguing with each other. It was the conversation that Dove had thought they were having silently.

First there was no privacy, thought Dove. Now there was no silence.

"I have never," said the psychiatrist, "actually come across a Dr. Jekyll and Mr. Hyde personality in real life."

"It made a wonderful story," said Dove's father. He was glad to discuss anything besides his child's deterioration.

"Did it really?" said Dove's mother. "I never read it."

Father paused. "Now that you mention it, I suppose I never read it, either. I was just told in school that it made a wonderful story."

"Robert Louis Stevenson," said the psychiatrist.

"I have read it quite recently, as a matter of fact. *Dr. Jekyll and Mr. Hyde* as a story is boring. I cannot say the story has withstood the test of time."

"You withstood the test of time," said Dove sadly to Wing.

"Only fifteen years," said Wing. "But that story was written a century ago. Neither you nor I will last so long."

"Of course you will," said Dove. "You're from the pyramids, you're from the Nile, something about you is five thousand years old."

"You know," said Wing seriously, "you have some very strange thoughts. Perhaps you should get some counseling."

Mr. and Mrs. Daniel burst into hysterical laughter and muffled it quickly, clinging to each other.

"Sometimes," said the psychiatrist, "when both parents work, and when the only child pretty much brings herself up, the imagination seems to gain more control than it should."

Dove's parents flinched. "This isn't our fault!" cried Mother. "We've been good parents! You can't blame this on my job."

"That's true," said Dove. "They have been good parents. And I don't blame this on the job, Mother. Listen to me! You're not listening! Wing was there all along, biding her time. Now when the perfume arrived, it opened the path for her to emerge. There is an antidote, but it wasn't very strong. I guess there wasn't enough of it, or we got into the car too fast, or something, but she just didn't fade the way she used to. What I need is — "

"I don't think I can handle this," said Father.

"There's no reason why you should," said the psychiatrist. "That's why we're here, you know. To handle things like this. Cherry Valley has a long and successful history of adolescent treatment. She'll be happy here. You'll be happy that she is here."

His voice was as soothing as syrup, and on the river of his voice, her parents flowed out the door and disappeared.

They were replaced by a group of doctors. "This will be a fascinating case," said one of the doctors. He actually rubbed his hands together.

Another doctor held a hypodermic needle in his hand. Very slowly he moved toward her, putting each foot flat and heavy on the floor. "Now, Dove," he said, and his voice matched his body: heavy and solid and forever. "We're going to have a nice lie-down."

"A lie-down?" repeated Dove. She backed away from him.

"We're going to rest for a few days," said the psychiatrist.

"Rest?" repeated Dove.

"Your mother and father cannot handle what is going on."

"They can't?"

"So you're going to stay here for a while."

"Here?" Dove had backed all the way to the wall. There was no place else to go. The door was blocked. A big woman and a small man with fixed smiles and extended arms stood in the door. Dove whimpered.

"It's all right," said the psychiatrist. "Nobody is going to hurt you, Dove. This is where you come to stop being afraid."

"Nobody out where *you* are is going to hurt me," said Dove. "It's inside my head I'm worried about."

"This is intriguing," said a visiting doctor. "What a treat to be allowed to observe this case."

The needle came closer.

I'm a case, thought Dove Daniel.

A mental case.

A suitcase.

A bookcase.

A briefcase.

The needle went in.

A basket case, she thought, and the world went dim.

Chapter 20

She did not know what medication they had given her, but it had an interesting effect: She was soft. Her brain was mushy, and her muscles were gooey.

She slept easily, but woke only halfway. The inside of the mind, already cluttered with Wing and Dove, was now also foggy. Dove and Wing stumbled around in there, each of them trying to think and to take charge. Their conversations were mumbled, and their thoughts tangled.

The hospital was terrifying. Creepy people walked up and down the hallways. Dove was afraid of everybody there. She was afraid of the locks on the doors and the bars on the windows. She was afraid of the supper tray with the single plastic spoon. She was afraid of the attendants, who were jolly and friendly and had too many teeth, like people in toothpaste ads. She was afraid of the sky outside: If it was bright blue, it might be the Nile, and Egypt, and Wing's source . . . if it was gray and dismal, she felt that her mind had turned inside out and was spread over the entire sky.

There was group therapy and one-on-one therapy and occupational therapy and even music and art therapy.

In group, Dove encountered patients with no inhibitions. People who would undress in front of visitors, or try to stab each other with plastic spoons, or lose interest in bathing, or talk about how they were really a king, or really the President, or even really God.

"Is that so different from you, Dove?" asked the therapist.

Dove was furious with him.

"You claim you have a second personality, too, Dove," said the therapist.

"It's a second *person!*" shouted Dove. "Not a second personality. There are two of us in here!"

The therapist beamed. "Anger is good. Keep yelling, Dove. We're going to work that anger out! Yes, we are!"

After each therapy, Dove was sent back to her room.

The room felt like forever. It had always been there, it always would be there, and it would always contain a prisoner.

Or two.

They did not understand.

She would never get them to understand. They had classified her with insane people. To them she was Dr. Jekyll and Mr. Hyde. A girl with two personalities. Dove and Wing. No matter what Dove said, no matter how carefully she lined up her explanations, the staff at the mental institute would not listen. They did not believe in vanished twins.

Dove thought the best line of defense — the quickest way to be released — would be a full and careful explanation of how she had gotten into this dreadful position. Each session she took a different approach. "Once," said Dove, "I assumed that because of our names, I am Dove the complete. The whole bird, so to speak. Whereas Wing was partial, and that was what made her so angry. She cannot take off without me."

"And now?" said the therapist, steadily taking notes. Dove could not imagine making her own pencil move so fast. Dove could not imagine doing any thing fast again.

"Now," said Dove, "I think Wing is the muscle. She moves. Whereas I'm the sort of the ultimate couch potato."

"How do you mean?" asked the therapist.

"I don't even attempt to get hold of the body anymore. I just lie here, up in the brain, watching Wing."

"But you're here now," pointed out the therapist.

"Only because Wing is still sleeping. This is very weird medication you've been giving us."

"Actually, Dove," said the therapist very gently, "the medication has been given to you and you alone, Dove Daniel. Nobody else."

Wing, maddeningly, refused to attend any of the counseling sessions and would not participate in any of the therapies. Silently, Wing informed Dove that she was not enjoying herself. *They insist that only you exist,* said Wing irritably. *Fine. Let them think that. I'm not coming out.*

How are they going to believe me if you stay in there? said Dove.

I thought you wanted me to stay in here, said Wing, just to be mean. *I'm doing exactly what you wanted a few weeks ago, Dove Bar. Lying low. What you have to do here is play their game, go along with their explanations, and thank them for their help.*

Dove wanted to kill her. How could Wing do this? Wing had invaded Dove's mind — her body — her life — her friendships — her family — and now she was making Dove look crazy.

Wing is evil, thought Dove. She told me that, of course, in the very beginning. But I didn't believe her. It's easy to believe that a person can be mean now and then, or nasty and calculating now and then . . . but evil?

What is evil, anyway? wondered Dove on the third afternoon, pretending to nap.

Perhaps, thought Dove, evil is your own body. You can't leave your own body. As long as you live, it's you. You can't set it on a shelf, or store it in a closet, or trade it in.

"No," said Wing out loud, "the body is perfectly ordinary. Epecially yours. You have a dull body, Dove. It's the soul, the personality, that is evil. Well, not yours. Your personality is quite dull also, it matches your body. I'm the one who's evil."

Wing was evil.

The day would come when Wing really would tip the gondola or jerk the steering wheel. Wing had come in order to hurt, and using Dove, she had the flesh and bones to do it.

"No, Wing," said Dove. "I accept that we have to live together. I accept that you're here. But we don't want to be a danger to others, Wing. We want to be *nice* to others, Wing."

Wing thought about this. Dove listened to Wing's thoughts. How complex and confused they were. They looped and laced around like tangled invisible fishing wire.

"No, I can't say that I want to be nice to others."

Through the observation glass, people took notes and nodded to each other. It seemed to Dove the whole world was nodding, but none of them except Dove understood why.

Dove asked, "Wing, what do you have in mind?"

Wing drifted into silence. Her words spun inside Dove's head like cotton candy. *Come. Let's lie down. You listen to me. I have so much to say.*

They lay down.

There was a single cotton blanket. White. White for purity, although nothing in Dove's world was pure now.

Dove drew it up over her body, and then over her head, and in the privacy of the cotton-lidded world, she listened to Wing's plans.

I need the body, said Wing. *You really don't, Dove. You may rest now. You've earned it. It's my turn.*

Dove looked through the blanket; close up it had a tiny, tiny pattern of crosshatches, eternally woven. If only her brain could be so geometric and predictable!

You lie down at the back of the mind, so to speak, and rest, suggested Wing. *Remember, you don't have to feel guilty about what I do with the body. It won't be you doing it! That's the beauty of this. Dove won't be responsible. I will be!*

Dove could nap through whatever Wing did with their life. It wouldn't be Dove being evil, or just being difficult. It would be Wing.

Give up, whispered Wing, as softly as a feather falling from the sky. *Give up, Dove. You have that choice.*

How tempting it was.

Fighting Wing took such energy. It was so humiliating to face the consequences of Wing's actions.

Yes, said Wing, *Yesss, yesssss, yessssssssss!*

I don't want to do evil myself, thought Dove, dizzy from Wing's insistent hissing. If I give up, am I cooperating with evil? What might Wing actually do if I let her have me?

Give up!

But — Wing planned to be a danger to others. Dove knew what Wing was capable of. She could not, in all conscience, let Wing behave like that.

Give in!

And yet . . . it would be so relaxing. It would be like lying in the sun at the beach forever; no body, no thoughts, just heat and wind. Perhaps that is what Wing was during the fifteen years, thought

Dove. No body, no thoughts, just heat and wind.

Yield to me. Give me the body, Dove.

Dove lingered on the edge, between submission and fight.

Yesss s s s s sss . . . whispered Evil.

Chapter 21

In another age and time, Dove might have stayed in that hospital for years. Certainly the doctors wanted to keep her.

But this was a day of recession and tight budgets and insurance companies running out of funds. The insurance would not pay for months and months of hospitalization.

Dove stayed only one week.

It amazed her that this endless prison, this horrifying complete robbery of her self, had lasted only a week.

She was still half Wing, or perhaps more than half, because Wing was working harder than Dove to keep the body when her parents came and got her.

They had never looked so wonderful. So ordinary and safe. She had never loved them so much. Oh, Mother! thought Dove.

She thought the woman coming toward her was the most beautiful person on earth, and the man at her side the handsomest. Their eyes, their walk, their hands — oh, how Dove wanted her parents!

So maybe we weren't the closest people on earth, thought Dove. We loved. In our own way, we loved so much.

Did not, said Wing viciously. *They don't care about you. They —*

Dove ignored her. She had not known it was possible to ignore Wing. Dove elbowed her way to the front of the mind and cried out, "Oh, Mother! I'm so glad to see you! Oh, Father! It's been so awful! Thank you for coming. Don't leave me here again, please!" She flung herself against them and folded herself in their embrace.

The embrace was real. They had missed her, too. She could feel it, the way their hands closed so tightly around her shoulders and their kisses landed so emotionally on her face.

Wing disliked affection. She squirmed. *I am a danger to others,* yelled Wing, but Dove didn't listen to her. Who was Wing, anyway? Some invader. Best forgotten.

Her mother's long thin fingers wove through Dove's hair and caressed Dove's cheek. "Feeling better now, honey?" said her mother huskily.

More than anything, Dove loved her mother's breaking voice: the throat full of tears and sorrow.

"Much better," said Dove. "I was just tired. I'm fine now, I promise. It was all nonsense, Mother."

Her mother's arms tightened. How cozy and warm a hug was. In a way, it was like lying at the back of the mind: so safe and secure, being hugged. Everything was all right when your mother's arms were around you. Dove hugged back. Don't let go! thought Dove.

Let go, said Wing. *I detest the maternal body.*

It was her father's turn, and his hug was so strong, it lifted her right off the ground and swung her around. "We need you at home," said Father. "It isn't a family without you."

His kiss was healing. The little warm spot on her face felt kinder and gentler than the rest of her, as if Wing would not be able to use it when Wing took hold again.

Father's car had a single wide front seat, and Dove sat between her parents, as she had not for years. Her father drove with his right arm around Dove's shoulder, and her mother sat with her left hand in Dove's lap.

This is my armor, thought Dove. Their touch and their love.

"Why did the hospital let me go?" said Dove. "I was so afraid that I would be there forever!"

"They explained to us," said her father, "that a patient who is not a danger to herself and not a danger to others is quickly released."

Wing stirred.

A moth striking a screen over and over, trying to get at the light.

A danger to others . . . those were the words to waken Wing.

Dove did not hit her head. She knew now that people thought that was a sign of mental illness. Fine, thought Dove, I'll figure out how to live with somebody buzzing around in my head.

It won't matter, anyway, what Wing wants.

I'm safe between my parents. As long as they're here, I'm here, and not Wing.

But of course, she could not stay home forever.

Teenagers go to school.

How relentless and unfair school is. The thought of going back to that building was as horrid as the thought of returning to the hospital, and the windowless room, and the group therapy.

"Will you be all right?" said her mother anxiously, that first morning of the return to school.

"Of course," said Dove. Lies, she thought. I have wrapped my entire life in lies.

They kissed good-bye round-robin fashion. Kisses each way, and kisses again.

It seemed to Dove that her parents' kisses would be amulets to protect her from evil, but she was wrong.

School was grim.

Dove was abandoned.

Only Hesta remained friendly.

Dove could not imagine why.

Timmy was not friendly. Laurence was not. Connie was not. The eyes into which Dove looked on, the day she came back from the mental institution, flickered quickly away. The chatter and laughter that usually welcomed Dove were muted and spent elsewhere.

Dove was alone in a crowd of her companions.

But Hesta was downright chummy. Hesta

handed her a pencil, since Dove had forgotten to bring anything with her. Hesta loaned her lunch money because Dove had forgotten that, too.

What does Hesta have in mind here? thought Dove. I nearly killed her and she's cozying up to me?

Wing laughed joyfully. *Dove Bar!* shouted Wing silently. *You admitted it. You said:* I *nearly killed her. See? You don't know anymore. You can't tell anymore. You don't know which of us is which. You don't even know if there are two of us, or just another you!*

Dove shuddered.

I've done it! cried Wing. *I've driven you crazy.*

Happiness welled inside Dove . . . Wing's happiness. Dove was shaking with horror, and Wing was happy.

What kind of twin are you? moaned Dove.

Wing said: *An evil twin. I told you that at the beginning. I wanted to live, you see. I was looking forward to life. And I didn't get it. You did. So I waited. I bided my time. And now I'm destroying you.*

But why? cried Dove.

Wing was impatient with her. *There is no why, Dove. Stop harping on the why and the wherefore. Evil simply is. Evil does mean things, because that's what evil is. I am evil.*

I don't want you in me! cried Dove.

You don't have a choice, do you? said Wing.

Dove saw that the class period had ended and that people were streaming into hallways and going on to the next event. She saw that it was two forty-five and school must have finished. What had she and Wing said out loud? What did people know or guess by now?

Dove Daniel walked slowly through the high school she had once loved and been part of. How quickly it had been destroyed. She smiled at kids who were coming the opposite direction, and some smiled back, but most pretended not to see her, and instead talked rapidly and loudly with their friends.

She saw them getting changes of clothing from lockers, for sports events. She saw them leaving some books and getting others, for homework. She saw them wave and kiss and greet and kid around with each other.

She saw that she was alone.

Completely alone.

Where she had been a member, now she was simply a creature to be avoided.

"Dove?" said a voice softly.

She was afraid to look. Who would it be, that voice?

"It's me, Luce. I'm really worried about you, Dove."

Dove turned. The face looking at her was full of concern and friendship. A kind face. A face the opposite of evil: a good face. "Oh, Luce," said Dove, and all her heartache poured forth in those syllables. "I'm having such a hard time."

"I know. Where did it come from, all this hard time?" Luce linked her arm through Dove's. Such relief to be touched! To know that she was not a pariah. Luce wanted to be with her. Luce cared.

Dove wet her lips, yearning to tell Luce everything: the vanished twin, the evil, the perfume, the venom. No one yet had understood or believed. Would Luce? Was it safe to talk?

Luce said, "You don't have to talk about it if it hurts, Dove. But it hurts me, too, you know. I'm your friend, and I didn't even see that anything was wrong! I want to be here for you. Okay?"

The loveliest gift on earth: being there.

I'm going to make it, thought Dove. I have parents who love me and I have a friend. In the end, that's all you need. "Oh, Luce," she said, her voice quavering. "Thank you. I — "

Do you remember, Dove, said Wing inside their head, *that I am a danger to others? Do you remember that you asked which others I had in mind?*

Life dried up. *Not Luce.* Dove begged. She could not fight.

Of course Luce! said Wing. *Why would I waste my time being a danger to somebody you don't care about? Or being a danger to somebody who doesn't care about you?*

Dove felt Wing moving through her flesh. Wing took over, seizing her legs and her arms, her feet and her hands.

Wing owned the body now.

What would Wing do with this body? To what use would she put these hands?

Not Luce! thought Dove.

She poured herself back. With tremendous strength, as if she were diving underwater and needed enough air for hours, she tightened herself against Wing's invasion and stiffened herself against Wing's venom.

Dove and Wing fought over the arm that was linked through Luce's.

We're going to take a ride in Luce's car, said Wing, struggling. *That little tin can of a car. That car so low to the road she can't even go over the speed bumps at your condominium. That little car that is an accident waiting to happen.*

Oh, no, we're not, said Dove. *We are not hurting Luce!* Dove wrenched free of Luce's arm and staggered to the far side of the high school hall. "Go away, Luce," she managed.

Luce burst into tears. "Dove!" she said. "What's the matter! Really and truly, I am your friend. You need me."

Dove clapped her hand over the mouth to keep Wing from talking.

"Oh Dove!" cried Luce. "I can't stand looking at you! You're having some sort of convulsion! Fighting with yourself! Don't do that. Don't pull your hair and your face. You look insane. Please stop."

She obeyed. The wish was Wing's as well as Luce's, and the wish from two of them was too great for Dove to combat.

She stopped fighting with herself.

Perhaps the strength of evil is greater than the strength of good.

Perhaps good does not even realize it is going to need strength until it is too late, and evil has the upper hand.

Wing had won.

Venom was in control.

Dove tumbled, dizzy, nauseated, falling to the back of the mind, seeing only a blur where once she had had eyes.

Wing said coaxingly, "Luce, don't be mad. I need you. I'm going through some real personal problems here. Could we go for a drive? I just want to talk and maybe share some of this."

"Of course," said Luce, lovingly. "I was going to suggest that." Luce put her arm around the body, but Dove could not fool it. Luce hugged tightly to show her concern, but Dove was not there.

Dove was dwindling away. The space in the back of the mind was more cramped and dingy than it had been before. She could not quite tell what Wing was doing; Wing possessed much more of the body than she usually did.

What is left to me? thought Dove. Do I have a way to save Luce?

Wing's laughter resonated through the skull like an electric drill.

No, Dove, said the voice of her evil self. *You have nothing. Certainly not a way to save Luce.*

Chapter 22

Even evil is subject to interference.

Hesta intercepted Luce and Wing on the way to Luce's car. "Hi, guys," said Hesta brightly.

"We are not guys," said Wing sharply.

"You're using your second voice today," said Hesta, laughing. "You did that when you were in the car with me. I don't know what it is about you, Dove Bar, but there's some sort of spark that really attracts me these days."

"It's called evil," said Wing, not missing a beat.

Luce pulled back a little.

Wing yanked her in again.

"Let's go to the mall," said Hesta. "The three of us. Who needs Connie, anyway?"

No Dove was present. She had drowned in the tide of venom, and she was floating face down inside the mind.

"My car," decreed Hesta. "Yours is too little, Luce. I hate being crowded like that. Plus I have a better radio."

Luce stopped walking. "Maybe another day," said Luce.

Hesta flung open the school's big glass front door. A bright blue sky greeted them, brittle as construction paper. Solid but easy to rip. The sun was so brilliant it burned the eyes as well as the skin.

The sun lit up the inside of the mind, light passing through the eyelids and coloring the interstices of the skull. Wing looked straight up. The sun was both giver of life and source of ancient cruelty. It could cause drought and famine of the soil, as well as of the soul. The sun shines on the good and the bad, the sleeping and the dead.

Dove stirred, feeling heat and color.

Wing said without speech, *One victim is as good as another. I have eons of time. So Luce postponed her moment. I will get her later. Today I will get Hesta.*

Dove seemed to be at a railroad station. Luce was vanishing down the tracks, getting smaller and smaller, until she was only a memory.

But she's safe, thought Dove.

She tried to imagine time as Wing knew it, time that lasted generation after generation, time for all cruelties under the sun.

Whereas for Dove, time had run out.

I never did find out who I am, she thought. That's what you do when you're an adolescent: wonder who you are, work through your layers of family and past, try to find yourself. *I found somebody else.*

Dove wanted to roll over, face another direction, but she seemed to be lying beneath a great weight.

Perhaps a bridge had caved in and crushed her. There was nowhere to go.

I don't even know, thought Dove, facing the terrible possibility at last, whether I am real or Wing is real. I don't know if there are two of us or one of us. I don't know if there is a vanished twin . . . or a sick girl.

The car sped along. Hesta's eyes flickered constantly over Wing, assessing the situation, taking care, while Wing waited patiently for her chance, as she had waited the first fifteen years.

Hesta was not evil. She just wasn't very nice. It was kind of a middle ground, Dove supposed.

But I was nice, thought Dove. I'm still nice. I'm just not here.

She remembered an unpleasant bumper sticker: *Nice guys finish last.* Dove struggled for life and breath. *If they finish at all,* she thought.

The stutter of the engine ceased. The car jerked. The seat belts detached. The door opened. Dove felt herself leaving the car.

They were at the mall.

This is where Wing came in, thought Dove. If only she would leave as easily as she arrived!

And then she knew.

She knew a truth as ancient as Egypt, as blue as the Nile, as certain as eternity.

Nothing is easy.

Fighting evil cannot be easy.

It can't be accomplished by lying there. Nor by wishing. Nor by feeling sorry for herself.

She had to get up and fight.

Kick.

Scream.

Bite.

Raise hell.

Named for peace, thought Dove. Going to war.

You cannot fight evil except by waging war against it. I'm in here. I just have to pull myself together. I have to stop thinking of antidotes. I have to stop wondering what that fragrance was that half-saved me those other times. I have to stand up and fight.

Hesta and Wing passed The Gap, and Lord & Taylor's. They passed Brookstone's and Häägen-Dazs. Hesta kept saying, "Let's go in here. Let's go in this one. Come on, Dove, where are you going? Let's look in here."

Dove gathered her molecules and her energy. Dove reached for her thoughts and her soul.

"This is where Dry Ice used to be," said Hesta. "I wonder whatever happened to that store?"

"It served its purpose," said Wing softly.

"Let's go in the new store," said Hesta. It was filled with rose-scented soaps, mauve ribbons, pot-pourri, and lace-trimmed sachets.

"No," said Wing scornfully. "It's a stupid store. An old ladies' store."

Dove struggled and suddenly she came together, and was there, and had substance. In the prison of the back of the mind, she began fighting to get out.

"Stop that!" said Wing sharply, and she hit her head to get rid of the buzzing and the banging.

I'm getting somewhere! thought Dove, and she

struggled harder, and finally took a breath and began screaming as well.

Wing banged her head against one of the huge pillars that circled the center of the mall and held up the high, high ceilings of glass.

"Stop it," whispered Hesta. "You look too weird, Dove. We're going in this other store so you can get a grip, Dove.

I'm trying, thought Dove, but it's slippery.

The store smelled grandmotherly. Hesta hauled her friend into the store. Sweet fragrance wafted up from a stack of antique linen handkerchiefs edged in hand-done crochet. Wing's hand and Dove's hand fought on the same body for the same reach.

Dove got hold of one of the two hands. She seized the top handkerchief.

"Lilac perfume," said the storekeeper, smiling. "I've always thought it's the fragrance of gentleness. Of serenity and safety. Of good times and loving families."

Dove was up and running now, and she could see through the eyes at last, and hear through the ears; she was halfway there. *I'm going to throw you out, Wing!* she cried. *I'm giving you back to the sky. You came down the skylight at the condo, and you're going up the skylight in the mall. It's the same sky — the same blue — the same evil. Wing — you are about to say good-bye.*

Never, said Wing.

Hesta said to the counter person, "Do you remember a perfume called *Venom*?"

"Oh my goodness, it was out only a few days.

Very poor consumer reaction, as I recall. No. People don't want a perfume like that. They want soft sweet scents, to make them feel romantic and gentle and friendly."

Dove pounded on the sides of the mind, biting at it, gouging it with her fingernails.

Let me out of here! screamed Dove. *Give me back my body and my mind and my soul!*

"I'm keeping it!" said Wing through gritted teeth. "Leave me alone."

Dove pressed the white handkerchief against her face, and their shared lungs — driven by biology and not by evil — filled with air.

Lilac-scented air.

Lilac sachets, too. And drawer lining paper. Scented writing paper. And cologne. The store was all perfume.

Wing wrenched free, and strode toward the center of the mall, toward the place where the great glass pyramid raised its apex to the sky. She laughed, with her ancient history in her genes, and her terrible future in her hands.

It was not quite an antidote, that lilac. It was a boost, a step, a strengthener. But only Dove could throw off the evil.

It's you who will vanish, said Wing. *Forever, Dove. I am destroying you. I am going to satisfy myself at last! I am going to keep this body and you are vanishing! My strength is too ancient for yours,* said Wing. *You can make me pause, and you can make me stumble, but in the end, I am evil, and evil always wins.*

They were beneath the shimmering glass of the pyramid.

Dove did not look up. She did not look around. She did not look back.

She did not dream of a better past or a better future.

She just did what she had to do.

Evil cannot win, she thought. Evil cannot always be stronger than good. I have strength, too.

"Take her back!" cried Dove. "I will not be owned by evil. I will not let evil hurt my friends and my family. Take Wing back!" Dove stepped into the cool tumbling water of the fountain.

Hesta was saying something, but it was not worth listening to.

"Go!" ordered Dove, and her voice was as strong as a general's at war. With the lilac handkerchief she waved up a wind, and on the wind she threw the evil that was Wing. "Fly away, Wing," whispered Dove. "You were given a wing, use it."

"I don't want to go," said Wing, but her voice was only a tremble on the wind, and the wind was going up.

Hesta was not the only one saying something now. A great many people had gathered around and were saying things.

They did not understand. Dove was dancing out evil. It was an important dance, and it had to be danced now, and it had to danced here. You could not choose your battleground, or combat evil safely and neatly behind closed doors.

"Go!" shouted Dove.

* * *

And Wing went.

She faded like a newspaper left in the sun. Crinkled, kindling that flamed for a moment, and then went up the chimney. Not perfume, but smoke. Not venom, but vapor. Not even evil. Just nothingness.

"Fly well, Wing!" Dove cried after her vanished twin. "I'm not mad at you, I'm really not. I even understand. But this is my body, Wing. Only one person to a body, Wing. Don't come back."

Wing was gone.

She passed into the pyramid and the sky above as she had passed into Dove's body, without other people seeing or believing.

I saved them, thought Dove. I saved Timmy and Luce and Hesta and my parents. And they don't even know. They will never know.

I might as well have burned myself at the stake. They will call me crazy and I will be abandoned.

Dove turned to face the music of angry voices.

Chapter 23

The school year ended, and with it, Dove's friendships.

The only person with whom she could really talk, strangely enough, was Mr. Phinney.

"Maybe it's because you understand the ancient world," said Dove.

Mr. Phinney sat comfortably on the edge of his desk. He was free for the summer from papers and projects. "It is true," said Mr. Phinney, "that evil is ancient."

And perfume is ancient, thought Dove. But the scent of lilac is even older. It is as old as gardens. I sent the perfume spinning back into the past, but lilac I kept.

"I suppose," said Mr. Phinney, "that we study history in order to understand the evil that came before us, and continue the struggle to prevent evil in our time. Evil will always assault the innocent. We must always be ready." He smiled at her. "You were ready, Dove."

"I didn't even know what evil was," she said. She

thought of the perfume bottle, its sensuous curves and glittering prisms. She thought of the *Venom* inside. Gone now. Both gone forever.

Hesta had spilled the perfume when she left it at Dove's. What little had been still in the bottle had evaporated. In the end, nature had taken the perfume; Dove had been left with a piece of glass. She had smashed it before she threw it away, so nobody would ever find it and be tempted to keep the bottle — touch it, wash it — perhaps even put other scents inside it.

Mr. Phinney and Dove shook hands when they parted for the summer, rather as if they were sealing a pact, and perhaps they were, because in all the world, only Mr. Phinney believed her story.

Dove left the ancient history classroom. She left the second floor and the high school. She left the year in which another person had lived inside her mind.

She left the terrible memories of an ancient vial of ancient scent.

She emerged into the softness of summer. The only smells were natural, the only shapes were ordinary. The only emotion Dove felt was pleasure: a good, sturdy, kind emotion.

Good-bye perfume! thought Dove.

"Hi, Dove."

It was not the voice of a perfume evaporated and a bottle cracked. It was Luce. She was smiling. "Wanna come over to my house?" said Luce. "Celebrate the end of school?"

"Sure."

They walked together. Nothing is better than walking with a friend.

"Isn't it a beautiful day?" said Luce.

It was a beautiful day. A friend had forgiven and come back for her, and weather hardly mattered in the face of such beauty.

Dove stroked the handkerchief in her pocket. Her fingertips ran along the soft crocheted edging, as old as great-grandmothers, as aged as a more comfortable century. The scent of lilac drifted gently into the car, and held her in its sweet protection.

About the Author

CAROLINE B. COONEY lives in a small seacoast village in Connecticut, with three children and two pianos. She writes every day on a word processor and then goes for a long walk down the beach to figure out what she's going to write the following day. She's written about thirty-five books for young people. *The Fog*, *The Snow*, and *The Fire* was her first horror series, followed by *The Cheerleader* and *The Return of the Vampire*. She also plays the piano for the school music programs, is learning jazz, reads a mystery novel a night, and does a lot of embroidery.